RAWHIDE EXPRESS

Hardluck Lacy, they call him. The nickname's fitting for a man who gets three years in the penitentiary after defending himself in a fist-fight which leaves his opponent dead. And the moniker follows him to his old stamping ground, where old friends have now become new enemies. But years in prison have hardened him, and now he's ready for anything. Or so he hopes . . .

JAKE DOUGLAS

◆

RAWHIDE EXPRESS

Complete and Unabridged

LINFORD
Leicester

First published in Great Britain in 2015 by
Robert Hale Limited
London

First Linford Edition
published 2016
by arrangement with
Robert Hale
an imprint of The Crowood Press
Wiltshire

A catalogue record for this book is available
from the British Library.

ISBN 978–1–4448–3041–5

Published by
F. A. Thorpe (Publishing)
Anstey, Leicestershire

Set by Words & Graphics Ltd.
Anstey, Leicestershire
Printed and bound in Great Britain by
T. J. International Ltd., Padstow, Cornwall

This book is printed on acid-free paper

Prologue

1877

They came for him two days after the fight.

He opened the door of the only completed room of his prove-up shack to find Sheriff Carney and his deputy, Marko Quinn, standing there.

The sheriff said, deadpan, 'Matthew Lacy?'

Lacy blinked. 'You know who I am, Nate!'

'This is a formal visit and I require you to truthfully answer my questions. Now: are . . . you . . . Matthew . . . Lacy?'

Feeling some alarm now at the serious tone and look of the lawmen, Lacy nodded. 'Yeah, I am, but — '

'Then you are under arrest for the unlawful killing of Thomas McDermott on the 18th May, 1877. Do you admit

1

or deny this allegation?'

'I admit I had a fist fight with Mac a couple of days ago at the Ho-down, but wha — ?'

'You used excessive force and he died of injuries you inflicted,' cut in the big, lantern-jawed deputy.

'Excessive force! Judas, he was drunk as a skunk and mean as a rattler, and weighed fifty pounds more'n me! *And* he had a knife, wanted to cut my ears off and maybe some other body parts. I knocked the knife out of his hand, slugged him in the midriff, gave him a knee in the face when he doubled over. That's all. He fell and didn't get up.'

'Because he hit his head on a rock and split his skull.' This was the sheriff, deadly serious now.

'Well, I didn't know that! It was just on dark and he dropped and didn't try to get up so I figured I'd knocked him out and left. I'd had a bellyful of Tom McDermott.'

The sheriff's weathered face didn't change expression and his eyes were steady on Lacy's. 'There was no knife found at the scene, Matt.'

'Hell, there had to be! One of them short bladed things with a fancy hilt. He used to carry it in the top of his sock — or 'stocking': that's what he called it.'

'Yeah, Old Man McDermott is still a Scot at heart, but, while a lot of folk have trouble understandin' his accent, he made it clear an' plain that if Tom had the knife with him — a *skeen-do*, he said, but it ain't spelt the way it sounds — he'd have had it in the top of his sock or his boot *in a small sheath*! And the sheath would likely have come out with the knife when he drew it, but there's no sign of any sheath, either.'

'Dammit, Nate! *He had a knife*!'

'I stopped off at a couple places on the way over here, including Dean Lewis's — now Dean's your friend and he saw the fight — but he didn't mention any knife.'

'Well, I was pretty fast, kicking it outa Mac's hand. But, God's teeth, Nate! It should've been there. Did you look closer — ?' He broke off when he saw the hardening of the lawman's face, quickly held up a hand. 'OK, OK, I know you would've searched thoroughly but if this is going to trial I'll need that knife. Someone coulda picked it up! It was a real fancy handle, ivory and silver. Mac showed it to me one time, proud it'd been handed down from his great great grandfather or someone.'

'But he wasn't carrying it when you fought him.'

Lacy started to shout but changed his mind when he saw the sheriff had taken out a pair of handcuffs.

'Gimme your hands, Matt.'

'Dammit, he started it! If he'd been sober he likely wouldn't've fussed. Thought I was 'stealin' his gal — what's her name? Donna or someone. I only asked her for a dance and she said yes, because she was sick of breathing in secondhand whiskey fumes from dancing with Mac. Next thing I know I'm

4

trying to swallow his fist and — well, it just went on from there. It was all over in about two, three minutes.'

'But Tom McDermott died, Matt.' The sheriff took his unresisting wrists and snapped the cuffs on. 'His old man wants a full trial and I have to tell you, Judge McLaren is a close friend of Angus McDermott's and he'll push for a hard sentence.'

'He'll probably want to hang me!' Matthew Lacy said, heavily.

'Could be. Better get yourself a good lawyer, Matt. I think you're gonna need one.'

1

1880

He had spent the entire journey from Larkinville on the rear platform of the caboose, sitting or dozing on his almost empty warbag, rocking and swaying with the erratic motions of the train.

Elbows resting now on bent knees, forearms dangling, he looked up when he heard the caboose door open behind him, tilting back his hat to see who it was.

The overweight conductor glanced down at him, juggling his papers. 'Might only charge you half-fare — seein' as you brung your own seat.'

Matthew Lacy smiled tiredly, reached into his shirt pocket and pulled out a folded piece of paper. The conductor took it, opened it out and read the cross-heading:

Department of Justice
State Penitentiary
Transport Division.

'Ticket's already paid for,' Matt said, 'but thanks for the offer, Hal.'

The genial conductor chuckled, writing something on the topmost paper. 'None of my business I s'pose, but . . . how was it? They gave you — what — three years?'

'Felt more like thirty.'

The conductor was sober now. 'Guess it ain't anythin' to joke about. Seems a lot for sluggin' a drunk.'

'Over with now. My 'Debt To So-ci-ety' is paid in full.'

'Wish you luck, Matt. You can do with some.'

'Yeah — well . . . Dean will've been lookin' after the place for me — just maintenance, you know, but it'll be good to get back, lose a little sweat buildin' something for myself instead of diggin' ditches for the State.'

The conductor was sober now,

busied himself writing on his papers and then, still scanning what he had written, turned abruptly and stepped back into the caboose, saying, 'Should be in by sundown. Mebbe run into you in town, Matt, sometime . . . '

Lacy lifted a hand without looking up. He wouldn't have seen the conductor's face if he had, as the man was walking away from him, but he had detected a *change* in the man's tone that somewhat sobered his previous mood of anticipation.

Maybe Dean Lewis would put his mind at ease when he met the train and they had a couple of drinks together.

Ah! That thought brightened him up. Three years without a real drink, only the prison's poisonous home brew. His throat was beginning to feel mellow already!

He shuffled to his feet, shaded his eyes.

Yeah. There it was.

That smudge at the foot of the hazy range: the Buckshots. It was his first

8

glimpse of the town's buildings in three years and he figured it had expanded since he'd been gone. He could hardly wait to wrap his fist around the first cold beer with Dean; the first of several.

* * *

It never happened.

For a start, Dean Lewis was nowhere to be seen at or near the railroad station when he alighted from the train. There was only a small crowd waiting and he might have recognized a couple of faces but they avoided eye contact with him. OK by me!

He smiled wrily. *Thirty pounds lighter, three years older but with enough added creases in his longish face for a man ten years beyond that and likely no one recognized him — or didn't want to . . .*

Well, he had expected that and didn't aim to spend much time in town before hiring a mount — if Dean hadn't brought one for him — and riding out to his place.

The dream of his own place had kept him going many a time in the Pen and in the hole, which was isolation with a capital 'I', a grave with bars, or riding out the dreaded Rawhide Express, staggering under the weight of felled trees for splitting into railroad ties, cleaning a blocked sewage tunnel, recovering in the pesthole they called a hospital after the guards had polished the toes of their boots by kicking him around his cell until the leather gleamed . . .

He had held the dream of that smallholding in the foothills, butting up against Dean's place, with its deep riverbend and one good field of lush grass. He had imagined a small herd browsing there in his dreams: it had seemed so real, he even *heard* those cows bawling in his cell! *Loco!*

And now, at long last, he would be able to reach out and touch that dream

— not just *touch* — he would be able to live the dream, make it a reality. Get on with his life.

He jumped when the locomotive's whistle shrieked and the couplings clanged as the train started to pull out of the siding, continuing on its long journey to Santa Fe.

Soon he was the only one left at the siding — no one had come to meet him. *What would they say? 'Welcome back, killer . . . ?'*

He hadn't really been on his quarter-section long enough to get to know many folk before that fight with Tom McDermott, anyway. Still, Dean *could* have sent in one of his cowhands to take him out to the ranch.

'But then it's gettin'-on round-up time; likely he was too busy and it slipped his mind.'

There were a couple of men repairing a hand pump behind the station building and, warbag slung over his left shoulder, he walked across.

'Howdy.' They barely looked at him,

continued working. 'You fellers know Dean Lewis?'

They both looked up, two middle-aged men.

''Course we know him,' the balding one said truculently. 'Can tell you where he is if you want.'

'Where?'

'Some other place but here!'

They laughed and Matt Lacy nodded slowly. 'Thanks.'

'Think nothin' of it.'

'That's exactly what I'll do.' Turning away, he paused. 'You know where his cowhands might meet when they're in town?'

The bald one spoke again. 'Try the Top Notch saloon.'

'Or Redhot Kate's,' added the second man. 'Aw, lookit that! He's walkin' away, not innerested after all.'

He heard their laughter until he turned a corner and saw Main Street opening out before him. He strode into it.

It didn't look a lot different but he

could see several places that had improved their appearance, with paint and small extensions. He paused when he was opposite the Top Notch saloon, jingled the few coins he had in his pocket and then said to himself 'Why the hell not,' and started across the street.

The bar had been painted inside, too, and there were drapes that needed laundering. As he recalled, the room held about an average number of customers for this time on a week day. Several looked at him, one or two stiffened, a few others carefully acknowledged his presence with a slow nod or lifted hand.

The barkeep glanced up in surprise, paused briefly, then said, 'Large beer and a whiskey chaser — right, Matt?'

Matt Lacy shook his head. 'Nothin' wrong with your memory, Trent, but a lot wrong with my finances.' He thumbed a few coins on to the bar top. 'Just a beer — any way it comes.'

'Hell! You got rid of that goddamn

pest McDermott — then took punishment without a whine. You don't drink house booze in my bar.'

With a flourish he set a large foaming glass with beads of moisture on it before the surprised Lacy. *Hell, he hadn't been all that popular here! Not since he was part of a brawl that wrecked half the bar.*

But remembering that old saying about the proverbial gift horse, he saluted Trent with the glass and took a couple of long swallows. When he threw his head back to do so, he swivelled his gaze around the room.

He was the centre of attention and immediately he felt uncomfortable. *In prison, you busted a gut to stay part of the scenery in case you were selected for some lousy job of which there seemed to be all too many.*

Once again, a few men acknowledged his presence with a nod, but no one came to stand beside him and start a conversation — or offer to buy him a drink.

But Trent took care of that, interrogating Lacy in his loud voice to what it was like in prison: did they have their own firewater? What were the guards like? How about the grub? And just living day-to-day . . . ?

'That's what you concentrated on, amigo,' Matt answered curtly. 'Hopin' you made it through the day — God knows why. The next day could be even worse. But, now and again, there were some pretty fair days.'

He saw Trent looking past him and tensed as he turned his head, and a big meaty hand dropped on to his shoulder and pushed him roughly back against the bar.

He looked into the weathered face of a bulky red-haired man with a crooked nose, and eyes that were pale and unfriendly. 'Howdy, Red.'

'Howdy yoursel'! Tommy McDermott was kin o' mine.' There was an underlying accent there, chopping the words, giving the impression the talker was throwing them at him.

15

'Sorry to hear it,' Lacy murmured. 'I found him friendly enough most times unless he'd been hitting the booze, which was most of the time, includin' when we last met.'

The redhead frowned, narrowing his eyes. Lacy was tensed for one of those big, freckled fists coming at him, but the man suddenly nodded, looking mildly surprised.

'Aye, lad! 'Twas the booze that turned him into a right bastard.' He paused, nodded at something he was thinking and dropped his hand away from Lacy's shoulder. 'Weell, many's the time I told him his temper'd be the death of him, one day. There's even a few times I coulda laid the heed across him mysel' but . . . glad I didn't.' He stepped back. 'I won't drink wi' ye, but I'm willin' to admit you did the only thing you could when Tommy reached for his skeen-do.' Lacy looked at him sharply. 'You knew he carried one?'

'Oh, aye. Some of us find the Old Country's ways kind of hard to forget.'

He looked around at the drinkers who were listening and watching expectantly — and rapidly becoming disappointed when the hoped-for brawl failed to eventuate. 'I'm no sayin' I'm carryin' a *skeen* m'sel, mind, but . . . ' He shrugged. 'Aah, let bygones be bygones, eh? Trent, another cold beer for muh friend here an' I'll take a wee sup of that drambuie you're hidin' under the counter. Uh-uh! Dinna say nay! I know my good friend and boss, Capin Jamie Struthers'd be only too pleased for me to have a wee dram outa his special bottle.'

'He'll cut your damn throat! An' mine, too, Red, if he finds out I served you his favourite stuff!' Trent seemed to have beads of sweat on his brow now.

'Aye, an' in his absence, I might just do the same if ye don't!' The pale eyes glittered and the on-off smile, showing a flash of big yellow teeth, did nothing to make the barkeep feel any easier.

But in the end, Trent surreptitiously served the liquor and swiftly replaced

17

the bottle under the counter.

The redhead led the way to a corner table and Lacy sat down with his fresh beer, looking at Red closely.

'I dunno this Struthers you mentioned, but I was kind of expecting Dean Lewis to meet me. You know him.'

The redhead's face straightened and he set down the now empty shotglass, wiped the back of a wrist across his mouth. 'Aye, I do — but, Matthew, my friend, I have to admit I say so without pride — as most folk hereabouts would, too, I believe . . . if they were game to, mind.'

Matt Lacy frowned. 'Dean? Why, as I recollect, most everyone got along fine with him. He was popular here before, mighty popular.'

'Aye, 'before'. Before he took over the Buckshot Range and the land of every poor strugglin' wee bastard tryin' to prove-up! Kicked 'em off, or made life so damn miserable for 'em they gave up tryin' to meet their deadlines.'

Lacy started to rise, but sat down, his frown deeper now. 'Are we talking about the same Dean Lewis? When they shipped me out he was strugglin' to develop his own spread . . . *and* doing it hard.'

'Aye, the D Bar L.'

'Yeah! That's what he called it. Aw, you must be joshin' me for some reason! Dean's not the kind of man you were just talking about.'

'Now, laddie, ye're dangerously close to callin' me a wee fibber — or a big *liar*! An' I canna stand for that.'

'Whoa! Take it easy now, Red. I — it's just that I find it hard to believe what you're saying about the Dean Lewis I knew!'

'I'm thinkin' mebbe he's *no* longer that man.'

'Well, it sure don't sound like it!'

'Now you be on the *whoa* too, laddie. I can see you canna accept what I'm sayin', but I'm tellin' ye, it be the truth.' He paused and looked around the bar. 'I can point out four men right now, who've felt the back of Lewis's hand and lost everythin' they'd worked for. Family men, three of 'em, too. The fourth's a widower and a bitter man. If you want *his* version of what kinda man Dean Lewis is, then you'd best throw a halter on your temper, or set back an' try to digest what to you will be *in*digestible . . . '

Lacy shook his head as the redhead let his words trail off. 'It's just that I — ' He stiffened, looked past Red's shoulder.

Red turned and suddenly tensed. 'Judas Priest!'

Matthew Lacy stood up abruptly. 'If I'm not mistaken, that's Dean coming through the batwings now!'

'Wi' that bully-boy ramrod of his, Bronco Cutler,' added Red Martin, sounding just a mite short of breath. 'Watch yoursel', Matt, there's always trouble when them two show up together. An' watch that land of yours . . . if it still *is* yours.'

'I was . . . hopin' but — Well, likely

not now I've done jail-time, Red.'

Before Red could answer, Dean Lewis apparently saw Matt Lacy and he slowed abruptly. Cutler, a solid-looking man in his thirties, a little over average height, with mean eyes, followed his boss's gaze. They approached the table and Lewis grinned: it seemed the same old grin to Lacy, but the boyish face behind it did look harder than he recalled. *Harder and arrogant!*

'Heard you'd come back, Matt! Sorry I didn't get word earlier or I'd've met your train.'

Lewis walked forward briskly, right hand out-thrust and Matt thought how prosperous the man looked in grey, pinstriped frock coat and silk vest with a black string tie at the throat of a cream-coloured shirt. Even a moustache.

His hand grip was firm and welcoming. 'Good to see you again, Matt. I won't say you're looking exactly fit, but you sure aren't carrying any excess weight.' He patted his own developing paunch and his grin took on a wry look. 'Can't say the same for myself!'

Matt smiled and returned the warmth of the hand-grip.

'Good to be back, Dean.'

'I would reckon so.' The rancher's gaze went past Matt's shoulder and rested briefly on Martin. 'You can go now, Red.'

Martin's face coloured. 'Well, I reckon I can decide that for muhself, Dean.'

Bronco Cutler was suddenly crowding the startled Martin, using his weight to force Red back a step. His hand was on the butt of his gun as he said quietly, 'You heard Mr Lewis.' He reached out suddenly with his left hand and dropped a coin in Red's shirt pocket. 'Get yourself a drink, Red, and go home.' He nodded towards Matt and Lewis. 'They've got a lot to talk over.'

Martin frowned, glanced at Matt who was also frowning. 'I'll see you later, then, Matt?'

'Yeah. Good talkin' with you, Red.'

Lacy watched Red go to the bar and order and the general buzz of bar room talk started up again. It had hung suspended for a few tense seconds there, hoping for some free entertainment in the form of a fight or at least a decent argument, but . . .

'Guess we should have a drink to celebrate your return, too, eh, Matt?' suggested Dean Lewis, smiling and taking Matt's elbow. 'I have a table here they keep for me.' Lewis indicated a small vacant table in a dim corner. 'Let's go get settled while Bronco brings us the drinks — still the same, bourbon and a beer chaser . . .?'

'I better go easy on the booze, Dean, been a long time . . . and that swill in the Pen — ' He grimaced.

'Ah, you'll soon be back to normal routine. Sit here and we'll catch up with what we've both been doing.' He took off his hat, revealing slicked-down brown hair with a narrow silver streak in front. 'Lord, it's been a long time. Longer for you, I guess.'

23

Matt nodded, sat down in the proffered chair, but felt . . . uneasy . . . somehow, despite Lewis's friendliness.

Red Martin leaned an elbow on the bar and sipped his whiskey, looking steadily at Lacy.

There was a clear warning of some kind in his eyes . . . *Go steady!* Matt wondered why.

Bronco Cutler sent the barkeep over to the table with the drinks and when the man returned ordered a whiskey for himself and another for Red Martin.

'Go on, Red take it. A drink on me.' Cutler pushed the shotglass along the bar and, as Red reached for it, gave it an extra shove, and liquor splashed on to the back of Martin's hand.

'Oops — sorry, Red, I — *Hey! What the hell . . . ?*'

Red had whipped his hand back swiftly as the whiskey splashed on to it and wiped it instinctively down his shirt on the right-hand side — just above his holstered gun.

Bronco Cutler stepped quickly away from the bar, and there was a blazing six shooter in his hand — two rapid shots and Red was flung six feet along the counter, eyes wide open in surprise for a moment, before they glazed over as he crumpled to the floor.

'God almighty!' exclaimed Matthew Lacy, leaping to his feet. 'The hell'd he do that for!'

Cutler frowned and lifted the smoking gun out to one side, looking kind of stunned.

'You saw it! Judas, the man went for his gun because I slopped his drink! I din' aim to stand still and let him shoot me down!'

Dean Lewis touched the angry Lacy on the arm. 'That's the way it looked to me, Matt. Red's a known troublemaker. Lives up to all that talk about redheads being hot-tempered. He and Bronco didn't get along too well. Must've just caught him on the wrong foot.' The rancher glanced around at the murmuring men crowding up to the bar now.

25

'You men know what Red was like — he's been in many a brawl in here. That's right, isn't it?'

There was authority in his voice, a brief hiatus, and then men began mumbling and agreeing. 'There you are, Matt. Too bad you had to walk into this kind of thing as soon as you come back. Ah, here's the sheriff now . . . I better go over and explain what happened.'

Matthew Lacy stood there, silent, looking a mite bewildered, but not so much that he couldn't see at once that the sheriff — a man he didn't recognize — was ready and willing to listen to Dean Lewis and Bronco Cutler's explanations.

The lawman made a note as Lewis spoke. 'Yeah, I told Red only yest'y, if he din' learn to control his temper after a few drinks I'd have him barred from the saloon.'

Matt recognized the man now — he'd been the town deputy when he'd been here before — name of Marko Quinn . . .

'Well, Quinn, Cutler's barred him for keeps now ... and Red hadn't even downed his first redeye!'

All attention turned to Matt Lacy as he spoke, grim-faced now.

He could feel Lewis's hostility like a knife-thrust to his throat.

2

BUCKSHOT RIDGE

The sheriff, barely acknowledging Matt, wrote a few things down as Lewis gave his version of what happened. He reached for the glass of whiskey which now held only a few dregs and Bronco Cutler grabbed the bottle and refilled the glass quickly, slopping some.

'You're kinda wasteful with other people's drinks, ain't you, Cutler?' Matt said quietly, jaw tight.

'Easy, Matt,' said Lewis quickly, and lowered his voice. 'The man's just walked away from a gunfight. I reckon anybody's hand be a mite shaky after that.'

'Some men's — mebbe,' Matt said quietly, holding Cutler's arrogant stare.

Cutler said nothing.

Matt turned to Lewis. 'If you've got a spare horse, Dean, I'd like to ride back with you, slip across and get used to my old cabin again.'

Matt heard Cutler draw in a quick breath between his teeth but Dean Lewis merely said, 'Aw, you can take a look tomorrow — no hurry. Come back to the ranch with me tonight. I've got a soft bed and a Mexican cook who'd make a vegetarian eat his roast beef and gravy and like it.'

Matt only hesitated for a moment then agreed, smiling slowly. 'Why not? My head's still clear and my belly feels at ease.'

Lewis laughed — louder than he needed to — and said, 'Got another bottle of imported bourbon in my cupboard at home . . . tempt you?'

'Sounds good. You going by the Buckshot trail? I'd still like that quick look at the old place.'

Lewis and Cutler exchanged a quick glance and then Dean said, 'Why not? We finished the cabin by the way — '

'You proved-up on my land?'

'On your behalf . . . sort of.'

'How in the hell did you manage that? I thought — '

Lewis shrugged and winked. 'There are ways — and don't worry if you see someone moving around there.'

Matt frowned, perplexed. 'Who'd likely to be at the cabin?'

'Well, what with round-up startin', I moved a small crew in. Wanted 'em closer to my herds on the slopes. You recall how steep they are on the Buckshot? Yeah — didn't reckon you'd mind.'

And didn't know I'd be back so soon, either, Matt thought but said aloud, 'No. Sure not. Thanks, Dean. Seems like you've been lookin'-out for me right well.'

Again Lewis shrugged. 'We been friends a long time, Matt.'

'Don't tell me *how* long! I'm feelin' old enough already.'

'Just one more for the road, then,' Lewis said, smiling, and motioning to

Cutler to pour whiskey into Matt's glass.

'That better be it, or you'll have to tie me in the saddle.' They laughed. Matt sobered as he watched two men carry out Red Martin's body. He raised his glass in silent toast.

* * *

Topping-out on Buckshot Ridge, Dean Lewis hipped in the saddle and leaned forward, pointing with his free hand.

'There she is — D Bar L — grown some since you were here, eh, Matt?' *Was Dean's smile forced? Uncertain?*

'It sure as hell has!' Matthew frowned as he blinked. *My God! The ranch was almost twice the size, judging by the placement of buildings and easily visible boundaries.*

'You've acquired a helluva lot of extra land, Dean, all the way out to the river now. Didn't Mel Hanson have that corner?'

'He did — I bought him out.'

'Recall you made him an offer before I left, but he refused. Uppity, too, as I remember.'

'Uppity don't get you nowhere with Dean when he sets his mind to somethin',' said Bronco Cutler, easing his mount alongside Matt's.

Lewis frowned at Cutler in what might have been some sort of warning and the ramrod straightened out his face, looking uncomfortable now. But Lewis merely smiled crookedly.

'I'd just made a good profit on the sale of some steers so Mel suddenly found that he wasn't so attached to that land after all. Made him an offer he couldn't refuse.'

'And how!' Cutler said, laughing, chopping off the sound quickly, as Matt looked from one man to the other.

'I miss some kinda joke?'

'No, no. Except you didn't see how fast Old Mel changed his mind when I named my price. He never thought I had that much to spend.'

Matt nodded, but there was some

uneasiness beginning in him. *He knew Mel Hanson had been mighty attached to his land because his wife of thirty-some years had died and was buried there. Swore he'd never sell, and wanted to be buried alongside her when his time came.*

Dean was standing in the stirrups now, sweeping an arm around the country between the river and the first of the Buckshot foothills. 'D Bar L goes clear up — and over — them slopes now, down on to your — what *used* to be your section. I aim to drive my herds up that way. It's an easier grade and'll cut miles off the old trail to market.'

He looked steadily at Matt as he said this and Matt knew why — and suddenly thought, *To hell with it!* He decided he was being bullied — quietly, but bullied nonetheless — and decided to make Lewis spell it out all the way.

Dean showed his impatience when Lacy didn't make the expected comment, then suddenly shrugged and gave a quick smile. ''Course to do that I'll have to cut across your place, Matt, just the south-west corner, but — '

'Right where I'd planned my best pastures,' Matt cut in. 'Any trail over that would *have* to go through 'em!'

'Now wait up! Don't get red-necked about this! I told you I proved-up on your place. I could do that because you were in jail and anyone who's served — or *serving* — time in prison ain't eligible for prove-up land. To save it slipping away into the hands of someone I might not want for a neighbour I did a kinda deal with the land agent.'

'What *kinda* deal?' Matt asked quietly.

'That I'd finish off the cabin before prove-up time expired and then, because the land already butted up to mine, I could put in a claim for it as part of D Bar once I made the deadline . . . which, of course, was no problem.'

'Sounds a bit like daylight robbery to me,' Matt said trying to keep the rising anger out of his voice. *This is what Red Martin was trying to warn him about.*

Dean remained calm, held up a finger.

'Now, hold-up! I knew you weren't gonna be in jail forever, so I made the deal, and figured when you finally got out you could work that land like you'd planned before the trouble with Tom McDermott.'

Matt's eyes narrowed. He spoke slowly, obviously trying to figure all angles of this. 'That was right thoughtful of you, Dean, but the land's yours now, not mine . . . I'd be workin' for you.'

'Well, yeah, officially, I guess, but it's still yours to work and I'll have my right-of-way. That should keep us both happy, right?'

'Unless we have a fallin'-out and you kick me off.'

'Aw, *Jesus!*' Lewis looked at the hardfaced Cutler, outraged. 'You hear that, Bronco? Goddammit, Matt, I never thought you'd figure I'd pull a stunt like that! Not on *you!*'

Matt smiled crookedly. 'Like you said earlier, Dean, we've been friends for a long time. Seen the best and worst of each other. I've seen you do some real dirty deals and seems to me this could be one of 'em — a cheap way for you to get your hands on a damn choice piece of the Buckshots just for the price of a little timber and a few hours' work on my cabin . . . and whatever you had to slip to the land agent.'

Lewis was obviously angry now. 'If that's what you think, then to hell with you!'

Matt sighed. 'I guess I'm a mite meaner in my way of thinkin' after three years in that jail, Dean. You've gotta be suspicious of everything — and everyone to survive — I guess mebbe I shouldn't've said what I did, but — '

'No — you shouldn't! It was a damn' lousy thought!'

'Well, look . . . I'm still not clear what you did to get prove-up in on time — and in *your* name. How'd you work that? They're mighty tight on changin' prove-up titles.'

'I had to do it that way, leastways, that's what the land agent said. He did a little dealin' from the bottom of the deck, sure, and it cost me a few bucks extra, but — Hell, I'd've turned the damn place over to you again, soon's you got settled in, if that was what you wanted.'

He's lying! Matt Lacy thought. Trying to cover —

'I don't think it'd work that way, Dean. I had a cell mate, used to be a lawyer, until he pulled one crooked deal too many. He couldn't stop talking about his deals, told me details I didn't even savvy or want to know about, but — well, you gotta have something else to think about except surviving years of misery in jail, so I picked up a working knowledge of the law, whether I wanted to or not. Pretty vague, I admit, but my land was on my mind in there: I knew someone might take it off me because, like you say, an ex-convict ain't eligible for prove-up rights. Fact is, I'm learning, he's got no damn rights! And, as I'd be in no position to complain, anyone could walk right over me. One of the things the lawyer told me was that if someone could fix it to get the prove-up rights transferred, then *he'd* own the land — which seems to be the way it's gone, Dean, whatever you're tryin' to say to make it sound like you done me a favour.'

Lewis and Bronco Cutler exchanged a quick glance and the big burly ramrod said, 'You ask me, you're damn' ungrateful, Lacy! Mr Lewis put his reputation on the line makin' that deal to finish your cabin for you. I was him and you give me that back-of-the-hand kinda talk, I reckon I'd kick your teeth down your throat then walk away so I couldn't hear you mumblin' for mercy.'

Lacy smiled thinly. 'Want to make a diversion, do you, Bronco? Change the subject by startin' a fight?'

'Why you son of a bitch!'

'Come on, you two!' roared Dean

Lewis. 'Cut it out!' He glared at one man, then the other. 'You are bein' kind of ornery, Matt!'

'Only because I've just realized Red Martin was trying to warn me that something had happened I ought to know about. But Cutler here made sure he couldn't follow through on it by proddin' Red so it looked like he was going for his gun. Gave him all the excuse he needed to shoot him and — '

Before Matt could finish — or prepare — Bronco rammed his mount into Matt's horse and both went down in a tangle of thrashing hoofs, tumbling bodies and the shrill shrieking of the mounts.

Kicking and lurching, the horses whinnying as they struggled, Matt dodged a hoof that took his hat off and grazed his temple slightly. It threw him into Cutler who swore and hooked an elbow into Matt's side, then grabbed him with both hands and *threw* him out of the mêlée.

Matt rolled and skidded, head spinning, grabbed at the ground to slow his momentum as Cutler stepped in, swinging a kick at Lacy's head. Matt rolled inwards, *towards* the ramrod, grabbed the boot and wrenched violently, bringing a startled roar from Bronco.

As the man twisted and fell, Lewis shouted at them to stop, but Matt rammed his head into Cutler's midriff as he staggered to his feet. He grabbed at the foreman's belt, swung him so that his feet left the ground and he slammed into a hip-high rock, the breath gusting out of him. Bronco's eyes were blazing as he lurched up and instantly reached for his gun.

'Stop that!' roared Dean Lewis. 'He doesn't have a gun, Bronco!'

'Lend me one!' Matt Lacy yelled, holding out his right hand, eyes glinting as they watched Cutler closely.

'No!' Dean snapped, as Cutler looked at some of the watching men, hoping someone *would* throw Matt a gun. But Dean stopped it. 'No more gunplay!'

Cutler glared and Matt, too, gave him a hard look.

Then the foreman shouted a curse and rushed in with fists swinging.

Matt moved fast but caught a blow on the right ear that made his head ring and his eyes momentarily cross. He got his guard up in time to divert the follow-up blow, the motion forcing Bronco to take a quick step and almost lose balance. He did lose balance a second later, when Matt hooked him on the side of the neck, drove a straight right into the man's contorted face, putting him down. Big and all as he was, Bronco Cutler was agile and he rolled on to his shoulders and surprised them all by making a convulsive leap that put him back on his feet.

Matt blinked at the manoeuvre and stopped a punch on the side of his jaw that almost dislocated it. He staggered sideways, felt his left leg starting to bend under him, fought it and made a mess of it. He was practically sitting — without a seat — when the big ramrod closed, lifted a knee into his chest, following speedily with rapid one-two, blows, taking Matt in the head, and staggering him.

The only good thing that came of it was that Cutler cursed and hugged his right fist against his chest: obviously he had hurt it, possibly even popped a knuckle striking Matt's hard head. But Matt was down and struggling to find leverage so he could get back on his feet. Instead, still rubbing his throbbing hand, Cutler stepped in and kicked him in the side. Matt rolled down a small slope which saved him from a follow-up kick and put Cutler off-balance.

He rolled on to all fours, fighting for breath, but ignored the pain in his side and lunged up. Cutler was bending forward, hands reaching for Matt's hair, and Matt snapped his legs straight, driving the top of his head into the ramrod's face.

Bronco's nose broke with a creaking

sound, and blood flowed, his thick lips were mashed back against his big teeth and he hung there without moving for a couple of seconds — during which time Matt Lacy set his boots on the uneven ground, hunched a little, and slammed a blurring barrage of piston-blows into Cutler's body. The big man stumbled for a footing and Matt kept driving forward, hammering, breath exploding from him with effort as each blow landed. He saw it all through a red haze and suddenly felt hard fingers grabbing his arms and shoulders and he was dragged back.

He saw that Dean and two other 'punchers had hauled him away from the downed and bloody Cutler who was moaning, barely conscious.

'Christ, man!' snapped Dean Lewis, now looking at the blood-streaked Lacy with his torn shirt hanging from his belt, body and arms gleaming with sweat — and blood. 'You'll kill him!'

'That's jail-fightin', Mr Lewis,' said one of the 'punchers, a rawboned man called Hawke. 'I've seen it. In the Pen, you have'ta kill or cripple the other man or some night you'll wake up with a shiv in your ribs.'

Dean looked hard at the cowboy and it was obvious he hadn't known Hawke was an ex-convict, but he turned back to Lacy, who had stopped struggling, panting as he looked down at the bloody form of Bronco Cutler sprawled at his feet.

'Must've been a real cosy holiday you had for them three years, Matt,' Dean commented wryly.

Matt didn't have enough breath to spare for a reply. He fumbled at his shirt which had been ripped to tatters, beginning to pull the remnants out of his belt.

'*Holy Joe!*' exclaimed Hawke, as Matt's body turned with his efforts. He didn't say any more, just pointed.

Matt Lacy's back was a mess of scars, obviously from some kind of bullwhip, but there was a section where the scars were actually formed in a symmetrical, checkered pattern: the contrasting neatness of the area drew the eye like the flash of a diamond on a dowager's wrinkled hands.

'Aw, boss, this feller's been through hell in that jail,' Hawke said, shaking his head.

'You know what made those patterns of checkered scars, Hawke?'

'Yeah. Seen it only once before in the big Pen in Atlanta: he's been through the Rawhide Express.'

'What in the name of hell is *that?*'

Hawke looked a mite worried that he had said so much, but under Lewis's glare, explained, 'It's usually kept for someone who's done somethin' like, say, stolen food, or medicines — anythin' that might affect the other prisoners in general. They can get really hot-headed about them sorta things. For some wardens, it's a good excuse to bring in the Rawhide Express, 'cause they know that somethin' like that is all that's gonna settle 'em down. An outraged prisoner is just as hard to handle as a wounded mountain lion.'

'Be nice if you ever get around to telling us what the hell it *is*!' Lewis growled at Hawke, who winced.

'Yeah, well, it starts with the feller that's been accused — no one has to *prove* anythin' — and makin' him run through a double line of the inmates — mebbe half-a-dozen of 'em have been given a bullwhip and some have lengths of wood, even iron pipe or knotted rope. They swipe at the poor bastard runnin' the gauntlet.'

He paused and it was obvious by his face he was remembering, and he shuddered.

'He . . . he ain't in very good shape after tryin' to dodge all them blows, but when — *if* — he makes it to the end, he's got another surprise waitin': two of the jailers are there with somethin' called a cat-o-nine-tails. It's a kinda whip with nine strands, sometimes with wire or stuff woven into 'em — the Limeys use 'em in their navy.'

'Jesus!' Two or three of the listening

46

cowboys exclaimed, looking a mite pale.

Hawke nodded grimly. 'Yeah. They's experts, sometimes actual Limey sailors, and they lay ten lashes with the cats — that's what they calls 'em — across the back of the poor son of a bitch who was just figurin' he'd gotten through the gauntlet and, even if he was hurtin', he was at least alive.' He paused and shook his head, mouth grim. 'Them whippers could pract'ly write their names with the cats and most do a coupla them checkered squares to show off. Marks a man for life . . . *if* he survives.'

He fell silent and the others murmured. Then Dean Lewis said slowly,

'I can't believe Matt Lacy did anything that'd make 'em want to put him through that sort of thing! He always had a kinda queer code of his own: he'd never steal from others in the same sorta situation as himself.'

Hawke looked uncomfortable. 'Well, Mr Lewis, I — I dunno *why* it was done to Lacy, but, like I said, nothin' has to be actually *proved* — an' — well, that's what they call the Rawhide Express. Anyone who survives sure as hell is mighty lucky an' *dangerous! Almighty* dangerous!'

Lewis signed to Hawke to relax now and looked down at the two bloodied men, Lacy barely conscious, Cutler out to it completely.

'Take 'em down to the creek and clean 'em up. Then we head for the ranch. That damn Mex cook claims he knows doctorin' and just about anything else you can name: he can take care of 'em. Now move!'

3

SPLIT UP

He'd had two full days lounging around the D Bar L house, recuperating from the fight — *he still ached like hell and moved like an old-timer with full-blown rheumatics* — but he figured two days were long enough. One thing about prison: it taught you to recover quickly after a beating, or you'd get another just to hurry things along.

Bronco Cutler was in the bunkhouse, they told him, a'bed in his partitioned-off section which was his due as ramrod. Matt Lacy had been pleased to hear that the man would be at least another two days recovering. *Take your time and suffer, you son of a bitch!* he thought with bad grace.

The boredom was setting in now and

49

he knew it was time to do something more positive. So he figured to borrow a horse from Dean's remuda and ride over and take a look at his old place: what used to be his place. He was anxious to see what Dean had done to add the finishing touches, wondered if they would come close to matching what he envisaged.

He had hastily added a rather crude and narrow rear veranda to the cabin. He'd planned — after completing it — to sit there of an evening, eat his supper off a tin plate in his lap and watch the sun go down over the Buckshots, reflecting off the bend of the high river there.

He figured it would be peaceful and pleasant after a day's labour around the ranch and by then he should have his small herd grazing those slopes: it would be good to see their vari-coloured hides bathed by the sinking sun . . .

So he borrowed a placid chestnut and rode across to the cabin. He had likely pushed things a little, he admitted, as pain trickled through his aching limbs and frame with every heaving lunge of the horse up the trail.

But he bit back his discomfort and leaned heavily on the saddlehorn when the mount finally topped-out on the rise and he could look down on his cabin.

There was a dull edge to his excitement as he remembered that this was no longer *his* place — he was an ex-con, so not eligible for Government Grant Land: he owned nothing here! Dean had somehow worked things so that Buckshot Ridge, and whatever stood on it, now belonged to him, or D Bar L as it would appear on the title papers.

Matt Lacy wasn't convinced that this part was entirely legal, but if Dean had greased the land agent's palm well enough, the papers would be sure to stand up to at least some kind of official scrutiny.

The chestnut was blowing from the

climb and Matt absently patted its sweaty neck, speaking soothingly as he scanned his cabin below. Then —

'Judas Priest!' he breathed aloud.

Dean had told him he had three ranch hands using the cabin during round-up, for his herds had grazed this far over the grassy slopes now that the ridge was actually a part of the D Bar L.

Those sons of bitches had turned his land — he still thought of it that way: *his* land — into a goddamn trash heap!

It *looked* mostly OK, he supposed, but it was the cabin's surrounds that knotted his belly: in fact, he could smell the rotting food and body wastes from up here. Broken plates, still with food adhering, had been flung out the door to land wherever they chose. A bucket he had made in his spare time, shaving and bevelling all the staves by hand with his hunting knife, now lay splintered in a muddy pool — he didn't want to think what the liquid making the mud might be.

There was more, but he didn't waste time identifying all the garbage.

He was unarmed, of course, but took a rusty rake with bent tines from an armful of scattered garden tools that had obviously been left out in all kinds of weather.

He growled deep in his chest as he shouldered the door open, but staggered as it jammed, with one edge dragging against the filthy floorboards. One of the thick leather hinges had broken and been left to dangle. This was the kitchen and he barely recognized it with all the dirty dishes overflowing the clay sink he had fashioned one winter's night, more food and broken crockery flung in willy-nilly.

The three startled D Bar L men were clustered around the deal table which had two big-bladed knives and a meat cleaver sticking out of the wooden top. They were playing cards and drinking — there were three whiskey bottles on the table.

'Wha' the damn — hell?' slurred a

ranny with a squint in one eye, trying to get to his feet but entangling them in the chair legs. He held a near-empty bottle by the neck, and staggered towards Matt, swinging at his head. 'Get outa here, you . . . '

Matt easily ducked under the bottle — though it hurt his bruised midriff muscles — and rammed the rake into the man, just above the belt buckle. He gagged and fell to his knees. Matt swung, almost busting the hickory handle across the cowboy's head as he dropped with a clatter.

By now the other two were on their feet, one short and toad-like, holding a whiskey bottle by the neck. The other was as big as Matt and he wrenched the cleaver out of the table top and rushed in, roaring an oath.

Matt weaved and dodged, swung the rake and hooked the tines in the grimy shirt. Cloth ripped as he grunted with effort and swung the big ranny into the path of the toad-like man. They tangled, fell to the floor, limbs entwined wildly as they fought to get to their feet.

Matt waded in, kicking the big man under the jaw, knocking him on his side against the base of the wall. He moaned sickly as Matt overturned the heavy table on top of both men. They spread-eagled under the weight, one struggling feebly.

Matt heard a sound behind him, spun in time to see the first man coming at him now with a broken bottle swiping at his face.

Lacy dropped flat, grunting with the pain it caused him, and heard the whistle of the ragged glass edge as it sliced air past his left ear. As the cowboy stumbled a little, Matt came up off the floor and the top of his head rammed against his jaw. There was the sound of breaking teeth, a strangled yell, and the man spread out on his face, bloody mouth slack.

The others were only semi-conscious, moaning or trying to curse. Looking around quickly, Matt saw a double-barrelled shotgun standing carelessly in a corner, snatched it up, broke it to check the loads, and cocked the hammers.

He leaned against the wall, covering the dazed and hurting men, waited until they showed some signs of being conscious enough to understand him, then told them, 'You miserable, filthy scum! Hogs wouldn't even live in this . . . garbage heap you've turned my cabin into! You can have one swallow each from that bottle, and then you'll scrub out this place until I say 'stop'! You want to argue, well, step right up, gents, I'm in just the right mood!'

★ ★ ★

He sweated and drove them until they dropped — literally.

The Toad, as he thought of one of them, was actually sick but, unsympathetically, Matt jerked the gun and said, 'Clean that up! Then we move right along and get rid of the trash out of the yard and buried in a pit. It'll need to be deep, too. You make it shallow and you might find yourself stretched out in it . . . you know what I mean?'

'Bastard!' gasped the man. 'Dean'll gut you for this!'

'That's between him and me. You worry about getting this place up to my standard — and you can start again — *right now!*'

Amid more moans and curses, barely moving with their aching muscles, they collected more soapy water and brushes and old rags and set to work — while Matt sat on a tree stump, calmly smoking a cigarette.

An hour later the trio were barely conscious, swaying with fatigue, watching with dulled eyes as Matt made his final inspection.

He came out of the cabin and went to stand over the three exhausted D Bar L men, shotgun held casually over one shoulder.

'Boys, I'm proud of you. The place is spic and span. *Shining*. Why, you could eat off the floorboards if you had a mind. You did a real good job.'

They looked at each other and, as one, weaved to their feet.

'Can we go now?' gasped the Toad.

'You can — Oh, after you do just one more chore.'

Groaning, glaring, they waited.

'What the hell is it?' growled the black-haired man.

Matt took his time answering, then grinned as evilly as he could, saying quietly,

'Burn it down.'

★ ★ ★

'You ... burned ... it *down*! The ... the *cabin*! Jesus Christ, that was to be my line camp! You gone plumb loco, Matt?'

Dean Lewis had jumped to his feet with such force his legs had knocked over the chair. His eyes were bulging and his nostrils flared. His breath came in windy gasps and he clamped a big fist down on to the desk top, some papers sliding out of a pile to the floor: they were ignored.

Matt Lacy sat in the straightbacked chair in front of the desk, not as inwardly calm as he looked, but his deadpan face gave nothing away about his inner feelings as he held the rancher's angry gaze.

'Why the hell'd you have to get your dander up?' Dean said abruptly and sat down slowly. 'Christ, I'd've had 'em fix the place up again for you — then fired 'em, if that was what you wanted. But now! I — I'm down three cowhands with round-up comin' on and not even a line camp!'

Matt looked at him levelly. 'Dean, I've had three lousy years living in squalor, with animals who called themselves men. I've eaten rat some-times when the warden decided it was too much trouble to feed us. I was whipped and beaten, even spat on. There was nothing I could do about those things, but take 'em as they came. But I *could* do something about the crap-house the scum you put in had made of my cabin. So, I did it. You don't like it — '

'*Hold it! Hold it!*' Dean was on his feet again, face dark as a thundercloud. 'Don't take that damn tone with me! OK. I took over your place: wasn't even your place once you were convicted. I figured I had no choice mebbe not strictly according to law, but I figured I could at least save something for you.'

Matt looked contrite — not too much, but willing to accept that maybe he was sounding-off unnecessarily. 'Yeah, I know, Dean: that Road to Hell again, the one paved with good intentions, eh? I'm grateful, even if I don't sound it. It's just — well, it ain't quite the same, being allowed to live somewhere was your place all along.'

'No. Guess you're right. Just the way things worked out. Hey, you all right? You look like hell!'

'Feel like I've been there, but I'm

making my way back, though I reckon I could do it better with a couple of guns of my own.'

Dean was silent for a few moments, then asked, cautiously, 'Not thinking of going after Bronco, are you?'

'Not unless he comes after me. No, it's just that I'd feel happier with my own Colt and Winchester.'

Dean smiled suddenly. 'OK! Let's get you loaded for bear.'

Lewis called for one of his cowhands and told the man to find Matt a sixgun with bullet belt and holster, and a Winchester rifle — 'and plenty of ammo for both, Laredo.'

The ranch hand left and Dean offered Matt a cheroot from an embossed leather case, which he accepted. They lit up and had them smoked almost halfway down when Laredo returned with the weapons.

Matt strapped on the bullet belt and holster but had to borrow Dean's pocket knife to make two more holes for the buckle tongue before the belt drew in snugly enough around his narrow waist.

'They sure honed the weight off you in that jail,' opined Dean Lewis.

Matt shrugged, and examined both weapons. Though they had seen plenty of use, the actions had been well cared for, kept lubricated, and worked well with little sloppiness.

The rifle's ejector threw the cartridges halfway across the room and the Colt's cylinder spun smoothly, the hammer cocking easily. Matt nodded to Dean.

'*Gracias, amigo*. Feels mighty strange having the weight of a gun dragging at my hips again.'

'Reckon so.' Dean studied him thoughtfully as Matt drew the Colt several times. 'I'm hoping to avoid any big trouble, Matt,' he said quietly, but it was unmistakably a warning. 'I wouldn't want anything to delay my plans.'

Matt looked at him levelly. 'You keeping 'em secret?'

'No-oo — not especially.' But there was a slight edge to his words: he would rather not have had to explain. 'I aim to make D Bar L the biggest — and top-spread in the State, running the best strain of beef cattle this country's ever seen.'

'And you needed my quarter-section to do that?'

Dean stiffened at Matt's words and there was a wariness in his reply. 'I thought so at the time, and it was available. This country's gonna open up in a big way, Matt, and soon. I aim to be in on the ground floor when it does. You picked prime land for your prove-up, with the deepest bend of the river over your line, as well as your own creek. Gave you more water'n me. And D Bar's ten times the size.'

'The luck of the draw, Dean.'

'All I'm saying is it's prime land — and I admit it was a real pleasure to move in on it when you went to jail. Not that I wanted to see you in jail, of course, but it's got the Buckshots to protect it from the winter storms and easy slopes for grazing. If I hadn't been in so much of a hurry when *buying* my spread, I might've peeked over the range and seen what good land I was missing out on.'

Matt said quietly, 'You've got it now, anyway.'

'Hey, hey! Don't say it like that, *amigo*. Judas, once they convicted you, that land *wasn't yours any longer*. I had to step in fast and — well, it seemed fair enough to me.'

'OK. I — guess so.'

'I mean, you being in jail, you had nothing to say about what I could or couldn't do with it, right? *And* there were certain people I didn't want to know what I was up to. You and me had been pards, so I reckoned it'd seem like I was just doing you a favour for old times' sake.'

'Smart move, Dean, but we'd been friends, not just pards.'

'The hell's *that* s'posed to mean?'

'I don't call it 'friendly' if a man takes

another's land when he can't stop him anyway, works it any way he pleases and don't bother to tell him about it!'

'You were in jail, for Chris'sakes!'

'Prisoners have a mail allowance — even a few visiting days. OK. I'm here now, but seems to me I've come back to nothing! Nothing I can call my own, least-ways.'

Dean Lewis looked uncomfortable. 'Look, I needed to make sure *one* of us held on to that land. You weren't a prospect, so — maybe I cut a few corners . . . But don't worry: I'll see you right.'

'What bothers me, Dean, is you did all this with some four-flushing land agent who could've double-crossed you at the drop of a hat — and may yet try something — in the way of blackmail! And you never bothered to even try and let me know what was going on.'

'Grow up, Matt! You *have* to move when the time's right. Someone gets caught up in the net and gets hurt — tough luck!'

'I guess that's the difference between you and me, Dean: you don't give a damn about anyone but yourself.'

'I sleep well, *amigo* — and aim to keep on doing so. You don't get it, do you? I've got this slimy land agent in my pocket. He got greedy and now he's taken one step too far and he can't go back. It's like having money in the bank, Matt, I can make him do whatever I want.'

'*You* want . . . ?'

'Yes! He had to do something to earn what I was paying him. If there's anything illegal, that's his problem: *I* don't want to know about it.'

Matt shook his head slowly, showing just a touch of a crooked smile. 'Dean, you are one real son of a bitch.'

'Easy, man. Don't take too many liberties.'

'It's just that . . . well, it sticks in my craw — you just going ahead and not even *trying* to let me know what was happening.'

Dean was tense now. 'What else? I

can tell something else is bothering you.'

'Yeah, it's you not backing me at Tom McDermott's trial over the knife.'

Lewis blinked. '*I* never saw any knife! Judas, if I had, you think I wouldn't've said so?'

'I'm not . . . sure. I mean, I know now how badly you wanted my prove-up section: didn't realize it at the time. Hell, Dean! I might've gotten off with a couple of months on a manslaughter charge — mebbe no jail time at all, if the judge decided self-defence. Instead, I got *three damn years*!'

Dean Lewis's eyes narrowed danger-ously. 'You're mighty close to calling me a liar!'

His eyes flashed and there was a murderous coldness in them that Matt had seen a few times during the War.

'Well, I guess I wouldn't want to do that.'

'Good thinking. I was you, I'd make a note of it!'

'Done.'

Dean suddenly released a breath that Matt figured he hadn't even been aware he was holding — then smiled. 'Hell, what're we scrapping for, anyway? You can still work the land however you want, and it'll be as good as yours.'

'No, I don't aim to stick around, Dean.'

'Why the hell you so damn touchy? Never used to be.'

'That was a different Matt Lacy.'

'Seems so. But — you really going?' When Matt barely nodded, Lewis said quickly, 'Look, I can stake you — glad to.'

'No, thanks all the same. I'll make out.'

Dean scratched one ear. 'Well, never expected this.'

'Me, neither. You lend me a horse?'

'Hell, yeah.' Then followed an awkward silence until Dean cleared his throat. 'Listen, Hawke told me about that Rawhide Express thing. The hell'd you do to get that kinda deal?'

Matt took his time answering: they weren't memories he wanted to stir up.

'I learned something about one of the guards I oughtn't to have. Thanks to that damn hellfire hooch they brew in the Pen I let it slip at the wrong time. To cover up and get back at me he claimed I stole medicines when there was some kind of swamp fever epidemic sweeping the jail. Three inmates died, and two of the guards. So us prisoners had to suffer. All — and I mean *all* — privileges were stopped. Lock-down was twenty-two hours a day. 'Course they blamed me and that earned me a trip to the Rawhide Express — damn near killed me.'

'You sure did hard time, *amigo*. You ever get a chance to square with that guard?'

'He was unlucky; met with an . . . accident.'

Dean smiled slowly. 'Serious?'

'Last I heard he was still in a wheelchair.'

Lewis's smile widened — a lot.

'Dunno what I was worried about: you're still the hard bastard I knew three years ago! You won't be wronged — ever — will you?'

'Good thought, Dean. I was you, I'd make a note of it.'

4

A NEW BRAND

He found the horse first, jammed in a crevice where it had obviously fallen after throwing its rider.

It was about worn out with its struggles which had lacerated its hide, stained one wall of the crevice with its blood. The animal's rolling eyes — *pleaded* — with him. It was the only word that fit one of the most disturbing experiences a man could ever have, in Matt Lacy's opinion: a doomed animal *begging* for help that couldn't be given.

The only 'help' he could offer this horse was a merciful bullet, which he did without delay, ending its suffering. The brand on the rump was a Flying C and he knew from his time before in this country that ranch belonged to someone named Casey. At the back of his mind he had the notion it was a woman — widow, or old maid, or something.

There was nothing salvageable from the saddle — not that he could check the bags properly, the way it was jammed there in the cleft.

He sat back and rolled a cigarette, looking up as he scraped a vesta across a rock. The whirling black dots were increasing in numbers already as they wheeled across the pulsing blue sky. He drew his pistol but held off firing a shot to drive them away . . . *what was the point?*

It made him mad, but there was no choice: the dead horse was there, and even vultures had to live . . .

Any more helpless anger at the situation was soon driven from his mind when he discovered the rider.

The man was halfway down the slope, below the crevice where the horse was. He had likely fought the mount once it went into its slide, trying to guide it to a safer part of the slope, but something went wrong and he had had to quit in a hurry.

Unfortunately it had been *too* much of a hurry and the man had landed in some jagged rocks. His dying would have been quick, though. The neck was obviously broken, one leg twisted like a pretzel under him, an arm at an unbelievable angle — and it looked like his skull had been hit with the back of an axe.

Lacy sat back on his hams, and thumbed his hat up his forehead. 'Hell!' he exclaimed.

It wasn't just a matter of prising the body off the bloodstained rocks. Now he knew the man had been riding for Flying C — well, the only decent thing to do was take him back there for burial.

'Christ! I always find the pleasant chores!'

★ ★ ★

Beth Casey irritably pushed some strands of her light-coloured hair back from her eyes and swore softly — but not too profanely — under her breath as the small screw she had been trying to manipulate into the tiniest of holes on the suction tube of the water trough pump, slipped from her grip and landed in the dust between her feet.

'For the damned *twentieth* time!' she breathed and sat back, wincing at the feel of cramped back muscles trying to unlock from the long, aching hours bent over the blankety-blank pump she should have thrown away before last round-up.

'Now I'll *have* to buy a new one and Lord only knows how long it'll take to get here from Los Alamos. They might even have to send all the way to Albuquerque!'

This time her cussing — though still under her breath — wasn't quite so mild.

She saw the glint of the tiny screwhead and stretched down to grab for it, but the small stool she was sitting on tilted, and she sat down in the dirt with a thump.

A ranch hand working inside the barn came running out as he heard her voice raised in real anger.

'Judas, Miss Beth! You all right?' He was looking around frantically for a rattler or something equally as lethal, but, gathering as much composure as possible, she pushed the strand of hair back once more from her face and told the cowboy, tersely as she staggered upright:

'No, I'm not all right! But there is absolutely nothing you can do about it, Danny! Unless you've somehow managed to come up with an engineer's certificate within the last few minutes!'

Danny, barely out of his teens, gave a tentative crooked smile — he was young enough to get away with it under the circumstances — and said, 'You know I ain't got brains for that, ma'am, but I — I'll do anythin' you need if it'll make you happy.'

She stopped her angry brushing down of her dusty shirt and corduroy trousers, looked at him sternly — but only for a moment — then forced a smile. 'It's kind of you, Dan, but mostly it's just my ill temper acting-up.'

'Aw, you ain't that cranky, Miss Beth. Not like your pa used to be.'

She blinked, restraining the smile that wanted to creep out. Then Danny tensed, pointing upslope.

'Rider comin', ma'am! From outa the Buckshots, an' — Oh, Lord! He's got a dead man draped over his saddle!'

Beth shaded her eyes. 'How d'you know he's dead?'

'Oh, he's dead, all right, ma'am — an' I'd say it's Harve Dixon — know that purple shirt anywhere.'

So would I! Beth told herself now, seeing two more of her men coming out of the barn.

'Looks like ol' Harve finally met his match in that big bay,' opined one of them, a big man, named Milt.

'Know that rider?' Beth asked, feeling a shade uneasy. *There was something about the set of the man's shoulders — wide enough, but kind of . . . hunched, like he was expecting a blow across them at any time.* 'Dear God! I believe it's that convict, folk are all talking about. Moved back to the Buckshots after he got out of jail!'

'That's him,' Milt said, with certainty squinting. 'Seen him at his trial for killin' Tommy McDermott.' He spat — discreetly — past the disassembled pump. 'Beat Tommy's head in with a rock.'

'Stop that, Milt!' Beth snapped. 'They said when Tommy fell he hit his head on a rock! That's not the same thing by a long shot.'

Milt shrugged, scowling at the approaching rider and his burden. 'Used to like a drink with Tommy,' he said quietly. 'Could be a miserable drunk, but din' deserve to go that way.'

'But that's all over and nothing to do with us — nor even that man, now. Lacy, I think his name is. He was tried, convicted and has served his sentence. I believe that anyone should be given a chance at a new start, Milt, he's trying to get one with that friend of his — '

'Dean Lewis,' said Milt, almost spitting the name.

'Yes — well, I'm reserving my opinion of Mr Lewis for now, but what I've seen and heard about him doesn't make me jump for joy that he's my new neighbour.'

'I've heard a few things about him, Beth — '

'Stop right there, Milt! We all know you like to gossip — and exaggerate — so — '

'Hallo, down there!'

She stopped speaking and with the men, stared as Matt Lacy topped the small rise and let his mount make its own way, while he held the dead man's shoulders so he wouldn't slip from his precarious position. 'Afraid I've got one of your men here in the worst possible condition.'

Milt and Danny hurried forward and slid the body off Matt's horse, carrying it into the shade of the barn and laying it down gently enough. The youth was quietly sick when he saw the man's head wound.

Matt Lacy dismounted, showing the stiffness of his muscles and, of course, the visible bruises from the fight with Bronco Cutler. He touched his hatbrim as Beth herself walked across, dusting off her hands and offering him her right one.

'I'm Beth Casey.' She looked past him at the dead man. 'That looks like my man, Harve Dixon.'

'I'm Matt Lacy, ma'am. Pleased to meet you. Your man died on a slope, way back past them pines that seem to lean over to the south some.'

She automatically glanced in the direction he indicated. 'Yes, he went after some strays up there.'

'Can't say I seen any cows, strays or otherwise, but his hoss had fallen into a crevice. Looked like he musta jumped from the saddle to save himself but he landed in amongst some rocks . . . with the results you see.'

'What were you doin' up there?'

asked Milt roughly. 'That's Flying C's land: not some free road or short-cut for drifters.'

'Slow down, Milt!' Beth said shortly. 'Mr Lacy can explain after he's had some coffee. It was good of you to bring Harve's body in, Mr Lacy. It's not an easy ride down from those Leaning Pines — 'Drunken' Pines 'most everybody around here calls them.'

'Was a bit rough,' Matt admitted, seemed to hesitate, looking briefly at the men and then directly at Beth — no doubt admiring her slimness which was shown off right well in the shirt-and-trousers outfit she wore. *In her late twenties*, he reckoned. 'Figured this fella should have a decent burial, and I — I wondered if, seein' as you'll be short on your crew now, I might ask you for a job?'

'Ju-das *Priest!*' exclaimed Milt, letting a big, calloused hand drop to rest on his sixgun butt. He looked at Beth and the recovering Danny. 'You — you ever heard the downright *gall!* Harve lyin' dead an' he wants his job!'

Matt stared coldly at Milt, swung his gaze to the woman. Her face was set in tight lines, and she frowned a little. 'Are you really that desperate for work, Mr Lacy?'

'Ma'am, I know it might be unseemly, askin' over a dead man this way, but — yeah, you want the truth, I *am* desperate for work. I'm broke, and I got no land of my own, anymore, but I can rope and ride.'

'You shoulda stayed in jail!'

Matt gave Milt a stare that might have meant anything. 'I don't think so, mister. Doubt *you'd* have hesitated once they opened them gates.'

'Three years must have felt . . . well, a very long time, Mr Lacy,' Beth said, watching Milt closely.

He was surprised but smiled briefly. 'A *very* long time, ma'am, specially when I didn't need to be there.'

Milt snorted. 'Oh! You was innocent, was you? Well, I was at your trial and it seemed to me there was nothin' to argue over. You killed a man, so you had to pay. You ask me, you got off mighty light.'

'Milt!' Beth's voice snapped and Matt noticed those pale-blue eyes had darkened with the cold look of a winter's night. 'That's enough! I told you earlier, all this is in the past. Nothing to do with us now!'

Milt didn't take his angry gaze off Matt's face. 'Tommy McDermott was a friend of mine . . . and you killed him!'

'It was an accident, mister,' Matt said softly, his face only inches from the startled Milt now. 'But you keep ridin' me, I could get mad enough to want to kill you and that won't be no accident!'

'Here! Stop this at once!' cried the girl, looking really angry. 'Milt, you hush up! You're ever the troublemaker, and I've got enough problems running this place now without you making any more for me.'

'You damn well don't stick up for your men, do you?' Milt growled, really surly now.

'When they're worth sticking-up for, Milt!'

'An' — an' I *ain't*?'

'Oh, for Heaven's sake! Milt, you can't do a single thing without making a fuss, stirring things where there's no need. I've lost some good top hands because of your niggling in the past and — I think I've had about enough. Now, you can take that as a warning — a *final* warning — or me firing you right now: the choice is yours!'

She was fuming and Matt saw her small hands were clenched into fists, the knuckles showing whitely through the brown skin. *He wouldn't like to be on the wrong end of one of those when she started swinging!*

He touched a hand to his hatbrim. 'Ma'am, my apologies. I never meant to start all these shenanigans, so if you'll just allow me to water my horse, and myself, I'll be on my way.'

'Hold-up, Mr Lacy.' She was speaking to him, but looking at Milt. 'I believe Milt's leaving now and as Harve has met his untimely end, I *will* be short-handed. If you can convince me you know something about working a ranch, you've got a job.'

'Why, that's right good of you, ma'am.'

'Goddamittohell!' exploded Milt, his eyes wild, and his hands trembling — but he made no move for his gun. 'You owe me pay, Beth! And I want it now!'

Beth Casey seemed calmer and looked at him steadily as she shook her head a little. 'I don't keep that much money in the house, Milt, you know that. I'll write you a note to the banker and you can pick up your pay in town.'

Milt's breath was roaring through his big nostrils, his lips were pursed and white around the edges as he looked pure hate at Matt Lacy.

'You won't last long!' he rasped, and suddenly swung away, heading for the bunkhouse, no doubt to pack his gear.

'I'm real sorry to cause all this fuss, ma'am.' Matt said. 'I say again, I had no such intentions.'

'I'm sure you didn't — and my name's Beth, all right?'

'All right by me — Beth.'

'With Milt going, Danny, you take a step up to top hand — and your first job will be to arrange a funeral for Harve. I think he'd enjoy being buried on Doughball Hill.' She smiled briefly at Matt. 'You may have noticed that Harve was quite thick around the middle: he lived for his doughballs.'

'Like 'em myself,' Lacy admitted. 'I thank you for the job, Beth. It'll be a good feelin' to earn some *dinero* again.'

She looked at him sharply. 'You speak like a Texican.'

'Lived there for a lot of years.'

'Well, the boys'll show you the bunkhouse and where to wash-up.'

She paused as she saw two more ranch hands had strolled across to see what was going on. One of them removed his hat when he saw the dead Harvey.

They both stared curiously at Lacy. Beth explained:

'This is Matt Lacy, we're losing Milt and I'm hiring Mr Lacy. Yes, I see by your faces, you know the name — well, he's paid his debt to society and it's in the past. I want you all to try to get along, and treat him just like another member of our crew.'

'Be happy if they just let me be myself, Beth.'

She gave Matt a quick look, hesitated, then nodded. 'That sounds reasonable . . . as long as you fit in. And I trust you realize this is a — a trial. If you can work cattle, you have a job as long as you wish.'

'I savvy that, Beth. Suits me.'

'Good.' Then she started up towards the ranch house — it looked like an old building to Lacy, but was in a reasonable state of repair, and still seemed solid.

'How long we expected to call you 'Mister'?' asked a man with bow legs Matt later learned was the bronc-buster.

'Just Matt'll do — or even Lacy. Fact,

call me anything — except late for supper.'

That brought a chuckle and the newcomers shook hands with him and then Milt stormed out of the bunkhouse with his bedroll and a sagging warbag. He curled a lip.

'I'll see you again!' he growled at Matt Lacy, striding towards the corrals.

'Not if I see you first.'

That got another small surge of laughter, as Milt stomped off.

'Seems like a nice woman, Miz Casey,' Matt opined as Danny showed him the washbench behind the bunkhouse.

Danny grinned at Matt's remark. '*I* reckon so.'

While he was at the washbench, Milt rode out — reins lashing and spurs raking as he drove his mount savagely across the yard.

'Seems a kinda mean cuss,' opined Matt Lacy.

'A bully.' Danny lowered his voice, taking a look around as he added,

'They say he was expectin' to marry Miss Beth when her pa died.' He shrugged. 'Dunno why — she never showed no interest in him that way. One of those fellers thinks women just can't resist 'em, I guess.'

Matt smiled: young Danny was quite astute for his age ... or a gossip-monger. In fact, the way the kid looked at Beth: well, maybe he hadn't *quite* grown-up yet.

To hell with it! Matt had a job now and he'd do it the best way he knew how.

Which was the *only* way he knew.

5

RANCH HAND

Beth Casey had a six-man crew, counting Matt Lacy now filling the space left by Milt Frazell's departure.

A couple of the men seemed leery of him, most were wary to some degree, but at supper on the second day riding for Flying C, Matt was pleased to hear a bearded 'puncher called Montana say, 'Ain't it quiet without ol' Loudmouth?'

Abe Dulles, the bowlegged bronc-buster said, 'Nothin' wrong with ol' Milt — long as you didn't have to work, eat an' sleep under the same roof as him!'

That brought a laugh and a tentative smile from Lacy, as he realized he was now the centre of attention.

'Can't say that I know the man — but what I seen of him wouldn't make me want to share a smoke with him.'

'Funny you should say that,' spoke up a cowboy calling himself Lofty, even though he was no more than five feet six tall. 'Milt was even too miserable to smoke!'

That brought more chuckles and when it had quietened down, Dulles, the bronc-stomper, said, 'I was you, I'd watch for more than steers hidin' in the brush.'

A couple of the others grunted agreement and Matt said, 'Thanks for the warning,' then added quietly, 'Thought I'd got away from this kinda thing when they let me outa jail.'

It was Dulles again who spoke. 'I did seven days once for destruction of property in a bar-room brawl, and I was a nervous wreck when I got out. Judas! The smallest things some of them prisoners took offence at! Like sitting too far along the form at grub time; nudgin' into someone else's space he'd picked out as his own by less than an inch! No way of knowin' till you walked into a kick in the *cojones* in the dark, or a bucket of slops poured into your bunk — while you were in it. Or you could accidentally nudge a man an' make him spill his coffee or grub. *Judas!* You wasn't game to close your eyes then! So I was you, Mr Matthew Lacy, I'd ride easy and keep twistin' my head to look in all directions — even if it did give me a crick in the neck.'

'Hey! Ease up, Abe! You'll have him quittin' and then we'll be short-handed an' have to work twice as hard!'

'OK! Laugh if you like, but you take note of what I said, Lacy. Milt ain't the forgivin' type. Beth firin' him has been comin' for a long time, so don't feel bad about that part, not that Milt'll see it that way.'

Matt nodded solemnly. 'I'll watch my step.'

'Now ain't he a nicer feller to have at our table than ol' Milt?' Montana said, and Lacy was genuinely pleased that all agreed.

★ ★ ★

He found he tired easily, was really shocked at the energy he had to put into hard riding and brush-popping steers, then fighting them back over rugged country to the two sets of holding corrals that had been set up. Luckily, the horse knew what to do, and more than once he had to make a quick grab at the saddlehorn to keep from being thrown because of the mount's instinctive manoeuvres, dodging and skidding to cut-off the snorting, lunging steers who had enjoyed weeks of freedom and now had to be confined or put into other bunches already rounded-up and headed for the branding-iron. And, eventually, somebody's dinner plate.

He had done it all before, of course, but three years' hard time in the State Pen did nothing to prepare a man to go from monotonous and brutal forced labour, day after day, back to the relative freedom — and damned hard work — of a full-blown round-up.

But he busted a gut trying his best and it paid off: at least with Beth Casey.

'I think I've made a good deal,' she told him one sundown while he washed-up outside the bunkhouse. 'I got rid of a liability and found an asset. Welcome to Flying C, again, Matthew Lacy. I hope you stay with us for a long time.'

'Aw, well, your cookin' ain't bad, Beth, so, guess I'll stick around for a spell.'

She smiled. 'Keep giving me cheek like that and you'd better start checking your grub!'

'Sounds like good advice.'

'Aah! Smart-mouth, eh? Well, I must say it's an improvement on Milt's gossip and troublemaking. But you take care, Matt, he may seem like a cranky old woman, forever complaining, but Milt has a real mean streak.'

Matt Lacy took that warning seriously, but it wasn't Milt Frazell who tried to kill him.

Amongst Beth Casey's remuda, Matt had found a sorrel gelding that immediately appealed to him. He couldn't put into words just what it was, but he felt a kind of instant rapport with the animal, some kind of mental connection.

Not that it seemed to immediately return any such insubstantial feeling, but it kept it down to just watching Matt's saddling efforts with a cautious eye rather than making him chase it all over the corrals.

When Lacy settled into the saddle, got off again and made an adjustment to the cinchstrap, the sorrel decided here was a thoughtful rider and likely worth cultivating.

In return for Matt's attentions to its comfort, the sorrel was quick to respond to decisive tugs on the reins and, later, the touch of spurless boot heels against flanks that had seen some rough treatment in the past.

Matt was quickly aware that he had chosen a compliant animal and went out of his way to encourage its trust as well as what comfort was practical on a round-up.

There was plenty of dust and yells, cussing and spitting mud, as well as tumbles taken by the Flying C riders, but Matt wasn't one of them. He came close a couple of times but the sorrel seemed to make an extra effort and he managed to stay in the saddle.

Matt worked as hard, or harder, as Beth's crew, simply because it had been so long since he had tackled this kind of chore, and he felt out of practice, but he soon got back into his stride . . . even started to enjoy it.

And then, on the third afternoon, when he was alone on a steep slope, searching for a trio of steers that had decided to play hide-and-seek, there was a sudden racket of gunfire and some wild, Indian-type yells. Surprised, he saw a whole bunch of cows he hadn't known was over this way

— although Abe Dulles had mentioned a restless group that appeared to be deliberately toying with the seeking riders. Now a tight-packed group of about forty came stampeding down-slope, trapping him between them and the lower slope.

Its edge spilled over a cliff about thirty feet high, dropping steeply to a boulder-strewn beach . . .

The sorrel seemed to take control: afterward, Matt maintained this, but admitted he was as puzzled as his sceptical listeners in the bunkhouse and couldn't explain it.

But the horse, instead of making a run across the front of the panicked steers, ran straight for the cliff edge.

Lacy was startled, hauled back on the reins, and found the bit was already between big yellow teeth and he had little control. He used his heels and body weight, swaying jerkily side to side, but mostly on the upward side.

The steers were maddened and he knew they wouldn't stop at the edge, wouldn't have time: they were in full stampede terror. Later he found that someone must have thrown hot coal oil over the backs of several, thereby spooking the whole bunch.

It was a deliberate attempt at murder — *his* murder!

But most of these thoughts swirled around his head in a flash and then he did the only thing he could: he ran the sorrel in a wrenching turn back towards the crazed steers. His gun was out and firing in a blazing volley that emptied the six chambers in seconds. He deftly holstered the still-smoking Colt, slid the Winchester from the saddle scabbard, knees clamped hard against the racing horse. He lifted the rifle to his shoulder, levering and firing so fast his hand blurred. But this time he didn't shoot in front of the ground-ripping hoofs, he deliberately shot three steers and they stumbled, their bawling lost in the general racket, skidding across in front of those behind.

There was a bellowing, kicking,

horn-ripping pile-up of bodies bouncing and sliding and tangling.

Three steers slid over the edge and two of those were apparently alive at that moment, kicking and bellowing, their echoing protests fading, then abruptly cut-off.

Suddenly, the rest of the bunch turned, swerved precariously along the edge, tried to get back past others crowding and sliding down. Another three went over and then there was some semblance of order and the remainder scrabbled and grunted and fought for footholds and edged to comparative safety. The dust was choking and gravel flew around like buckshot.

Lacy watched, sweating, chest heaving with deep breaths, and found his hands were shaking as he sheathed the hot Winchester. When he saw how close to the edge he had come, he felt sick, but more relieved than he could ever remember.

The sorrel was prancing, wild-eyed

and scrambling away from the now crumbly cliff-edge and he let it have its head.

As he reached a safe area, he glanced up, saw the freshly torn-up brush where the steers had burst through and glimpsed a rider higher up: a man in a checkered shirt and a flat-crowned grey hat, a rifle butt resting on one leg.

Just like the outfit worn by one of Dean Lewis's hardcases, a man named Fargo, he thought: Jake Fargo.

* * *

Beth Casey looked across the bunk-house at the sweaty and dishevelled Lacy.

'Have you — did you have any trouble with this Fargo when you were more friendly with Dean Lewis?'

Matt shook his head. 'No, nothin' you could call real trouble. Fargo and a couple others are Dean's stirrers, and Fargo's not the kind to wait for some personal reason to go after someone.

All Dean has to do is hint what he wants done and he'll do it, or maybe improvise.'

She frowned. 'Why would Lewis want to kill you? I don't like to be so blunt, but it's the only way of putting it, from what you described happened up at Mohawk Bluff.'

Matt hesitated. 'I . . . dunno, when you get right down to it. It's something to do with him taking over my prove-up section, I think. You can't usually get a transfer very easily, but it's possible, I guess, seein' as I was in jail and so no longer qualified for government grants. Dean did some kinda sharp deal with a bent lawyer — I dunno any details, but he seems to think he might be more certain of keeping his right to the land if I was dead. It's only an impression I got, have to admit that, but Dean's changed since I was away and . . . ' He shrugged. 'After all that, I have to say I don't really know *why* Dean Lewis would want to see me dead . . . *if* he does and I'm not over-reacting.'

'He was once your good friend, wasn't he?'

Matt barely nodded. 'Thought he still was, but . . .'

'And you feel certain that this Fargo must have been acting on orders?'

'Can't figure it any other way.'

'Well, it certainly seems like you were meant to either get trampled by that stampede, or be driven over the cliff. Either way would have been fatal . . . and still look accidental.'

'You'll never be able to prove that!' cut in the bearded Montana who, with Lofty and young Danny, were in the group listening to Matt's story.

'No,' agreed Lacy.

Beth frowned more deeply as she saw a sadness behind Matt's eyes — fleeting, maybe, but it was there. 'You and Dean Lewis have had a falling-out, I take it,' she said quietly.

'You could call it that. I never expected to come out and find my land waitin' for me. Jail ended all hope of that, but I guess I'm more disappointed than riled. Dean kinda *threw* it in my face: I could work my old place, but it was *his* now — and I'd have to do what I was told.'

'Well, that does seem reasonable enough . . . doesn't it? Or am I missing something?'

Matt took his time answering. 'Dean's changed, like I said earlier. He *wanted* that land long before I had the trouble with Tom McDermott. I'm not sure why, but I had lots of time to think about things in the Pen and I couldn't help wondering if Dean never mentioned Tommy trying to kill me with a knife in our fight because — well, so there was a better chance I'd get a jail sentence — a long one.'

'And give him a chance to take over the land which butts up against his place,' Montana said. 'But why'd he want that small parcel of land when he already owned half the damn mountain?'

'I dunno. All I know is he couldn't touch it if I proved-up by the deadline, but there was no chance of that once I was jailed.'

'Which left the land available again, because anyone who has served prison time is not eligible for Grant Land!' Beth sounded excited. 'But why does he want it? As Montana says, it's not very large compared to what Dean Lewis already owns. Is it more fertile, better watered?'

Matt shook his head. 'He's got some plans for it, but never told me what they are. Got me an idea they ain't quite legal. Pretty sure there's something not right about whatever he's got in mind.' He shrugged again. 'Well, I guess it don't matter now — he's got the land, legally or otherwise, and he can put in Fargo or some other of his men to work it and do whatever he likes with it.'

She looked at him carefully. 'You sound bitter. I know that's understandable, but do you feel betrayed?'

He was silent a short time. 'I must be pushin' thirty, I reckon, by now, and I don't want to sound like no pouting kid, but — truth is, I feel kinda hurt.'

He bit off the word as if it was distasteful and looked embarrassed.

'Well, there's nothing childish about being upset because someone you thought of as a friend has turned out to be less than friendly. In fact, downright unfriendly.'

He felt his cheeks growing hot: *this damn woman — No! Don't call her that, just 'this woman' — she was mighty smart and he found it uncomfortable, especially as he had grown used to keeping his thoughts to himself in prison.*

That was one place where nobody but a fool looked for 'understanding'.

'He got his hands on that land by some kinda sharp deal he made with this lawyer he hired. I think it's pretty much watertight and Dean's grown cocky. More or less told me to take it or leave it, and, readin' between the lines, not to expect any backing from him . . . not after I burned the cabin.' He paused, shaking his head once at some thought that drifted into his mind. He looked around at the others. 'We'd been *friends* as well as pards, but he was telling me he was running things now and he didn't need me any longer — if he ever had! I'd be wise to stick to my own business no matter what.' He paused again, looked at them squarely. 'Yeah, you could say I feel *betrayed*. I don't want nothin' from him, but after three years in that jail, looking forward to coming back to who I thought was my best friend . . . ' He made a kind of helpless gesture with his right hand, forced a fleeting smile. 'Kid's stuff. But I'd looked up to Dean for years, we'd been through a lot, and it was just as if he was sayin', 'Why the hell didn't you stay in jail? Or at least stay away from me . . . ''

'Well, like you say, you just comin' outa jail, you no longer had claim to that land,' growled Montana. 'Dress it up any way you like, but, in my book, the son of a bitch *stole* that land from you just the same! That's all I gotta say.'

Abe Dulles nodded in slow agreement. 'Matt, you've landed yourself between a rock and a hard place.'

'Tell me something I don't know,' Matt said with quiet bitterness. 'And I've been there before.'

'Seems to me,' said Beth quietly, 'the next question is 'What can be done about it?''

'When I look in the shavin' mirror,' Matt said quietly with a crooked smile, 'I check to see if there's any signs of grey in my hair. There ain't, though I feel there should be, the time I've spent worrying about that same question . . . '

'No answers?' asked Dulles.

Matt shook his head. 'None.'

6

MAN TO MAN

'Just what is the story where you and Dean Lewis are concerned?'

Matt Lacy was giving his sorrel a rub-down after washing some of the accumulated dust and dead leaves from its coat. He was in the shade of a tree down past Beth's corrals with two buckets of water, one soapy, one plain. Sweat dripping from his jawline, he finished wiping off the horse.

He gave it a pat under one ear, and was playfully jolted, nuzzled and pushed almost off his feet, but he calmed the animal down, looked across its back at the girl.

She frowned briefly. 'If it's none of my business . . . ?' she started and then added, 'Well, I know it isn't, I suppose, but — '

'Nothing much to tell, that's all.'

She moved her head slowly, back and forth. 'I hope you're not too touchy about being called a — a fibber but I think I've just decided you must be.'

He gave a brief, barely audible laugh. 'I've never actually shot a man for calling me a liar — beat his brains out, mebbe, or kicked his tail clear over the nearest mountain top, but I s'pose I'd better not break the rules and shoot a woman for it.'

'I'd be very grateful if you didn't.'

He had taken his tobacco sack and papers from his shirt pocket now and motioned towards a log in the shade. They both sat down and when he had the cigarette burning he shrugged.

'Like I said, not much to tell. We met during the last year of the war, two of the few survivors of the Pelican Rock Massacre.'

She drew in a sharp breath, horrified. 'Why that — that was a terrible *slaughterhouse* by all accounts!'

'Good word for it. Yankees botched

the last of it or we'd've been just two more killed along with the other three-hundred-and-twenty-nine Rebs. There were only about twenty of us left and we didn't waste any time getting out of there when we had the chance . . . '

His face took on a strange look and he spoke as if he was in real pain, remembering.

'I jumped some Yankee captain who was swinging his sabre, trying to account for a few more of us on his way out, knocked him off his horse and got aboard. The hoss was skittish and frightened, of course, with all the shootin' going on. Then Dean Lewis jumped up from a pile of dead men where he'd been hiding, got a hold on the bridle and ran alongside me, yelling 'Make room! Make room!'

'I didn't know if he meant the running men or me, but I reached down and he almost dragged me from the saddle climbin' my arm and swung up behind. We were nearly blinded by the gunsmoke still hanging in the air

— it was like a section of the sky had fallen in — but we got through into timber, dodged a bit more rifle fire and a couple of bursts from their Gatling gun. Luckily, they'd used up nearly all the ammo for it, so we got through and made for the hills and hid out for the last couple weeks of the war.'

'That surely must've been nerve-racking.'

'Not as relaxing as dangling a fishing line into a stream in the Piney Woods,' he admitted wryly. 'But we managed to stay alive and keep out of sight until they spotted us on a mountain there they call The Shotglass.'

'Oh, my Lord! I — I've seen that mountain! How well-named it is: just like an upturned shotglass. The steep sides are almost vertical. They say it's never been successfully climbed.'

'I'm here to tell you different.'

She stared incredulously. 'You — you actually *climbed that mountain...*?'

'Yeah. Amazing how much strength and downright orneriness a man can call up when he's got a Yankee mounted column throwin' everything that'll shoot at him. I guess neither of us, to this day, know *how* we did it: specially as Dean ain't keen on heights. But with a couple of boosts — or 'boots' mebbe, in the backside — we made it. There was just nowhere else to go but *up*. So we went.'

He paused to shake his head again, amazed even now at the memory. 'Right to the very top. They wasted ammo for two days trying to reach us, then something happened. There was a flurry of riders comin' and goin' down there and next thing the whole damn camp had gone, left abandoned, tents, supplies and all. We thought somethin' must've panicked them — and we were right, come to think about it now.'

'Was it really a retreat — not just some ploy to bring you down?'

He smiled briefly. 'Sure you ain't got some Yankee blood in your veins?' He sighed. 'Yeah, of course, they'd set a trap, left a dozen men behind, hid-out, to make sure when we finally did come down we'd get a big Yankee welcome.'

'Well, obviously, you survived.'

'Just. I had a bit of a problem with Dean: like I said, he wasn't happy with heights and we almost went off the edge. I got his hand just as he let go, couldn't hold on any longer. Then he nearly crushed me to death in a grateful hug . . . and that nearly put us over the side anyway!' He grinned, a mite embarrassed at trying to make little of what were really true heroics.

'We got down safely, but only because those Yankees got word that it was only a matter of hours before the surrender of the Confederates and — well, I guess the commanding officer said, 'To hell with it! Why risk a bullet this close to the end? Let's go home, boys!' Something like that.

'And they left, the whole she-bang. Just up and quit, rode out and left a cloud of dust that stayed there for an hour they were in such a hurry. They'd've got us if they'd hung on for a little longer — see, we were both wounded.'

'Dear God.' Beth's voice was hushed. 'And you'd climbed that *unclimbable* mountain. Up *and* down. How bad were your wounds?'

He shrugged. 'A ball had creased Dean's skull and another his hip — left one, I think — don't matter. It cramped up his muscles some but he could still walk — sorta 'stagger', I guess, is better.'

'And you? Where were you hit?'

'I caught a ricochet in the side, just above my belt — just as the Yankees were leaving. Likely one of the last shots of the war. 'Hardluck Lacy' they dubbed me. It busted a couple of ribs and hurt like hell to breathe. Dean was stumblin', complaining of a mighty bad headache. I had to steady him a couple of times, he weaved so much, and then we got on to a dead tree and, hidin' among the branches, floated downriver a'ways till we washed ashore. Neither of us had any strength to go on: I guess we must've passed out for a bit.

'It rained heavily again, we got goin', helping each other, and came to a flooded creek. I had no hope of swimmin' with my ribs the way they were. We had no grub but we waited a day till the creek settled down some and then I sort of hung on to Dean's belt, locking my hands underneath it, and he got me across that way, him carrying me for a while, then me draggin' him. Half a day later, we stumbled into a Confederate camp where we found out the war had really ended.'

She was looking at him with a puzzled expression.

'You changed your tone just then. Was there something wrong after all?'

He took his time answering. 'Not right then. There was plenty of celebration in the camp, and lots of civilians with the soldiers, some from what they called the Press Corps.'

'Oh yes, of course! The reporters from the various magazines and newspapers. I've heard it was very competitive at times, all looking for sensational stories, some actually coming to blows trying to get interviews with our soldiers.'

'Yeah, some got a bit carried away. It was pretty wild. They all wanted personal stories, especially escape from the Yankees with lots of close shaves.'

'You were able to give them such a story, of course.'

'Well, we were both wounded, but Dean — I forgot to mention he was a non-com, a sergeant, second-class — appeared in the story when it was printed as 'an officer' who carried one of his *severely* wounded men — me — through hostile Yankee territory on his back for most of forty miles.'

'*Forty miles*! I thought you said he'd just gotten you across that creek, you holding on to his belt.'

'That's it — forty *yards* mebbe, but those reporters wanted *sensation*. The South needed something to hang on to. We'd lost the damn war so any story about Johnny Rebs outwitting the Yankees or working through their lines

— especially *wounded Rebs*, you know, 'hero-types' — well, it gave 'em something of a boost, like a bit of sugar with the castor oil.' He paused and cleared his throat.

'And that colonel wasn't averse to publicity, either, and on the strength of the forty *miles*, he recommended Dean for a medal for his bravery. 'Our men were heroes to the last, defiant, loyal to the defeated South and each other, as they escaped together from the Yankee devils', . . . you know the kind of thing.'

'Dean never spoke up?' Beth asked, and Matt shook his head.

'Why would he? No point in him stepping back from a chance at fame and glory.'

'But that's totally unfair!' She stared hard. 'You saved Dean's life as much as he saved yours! *More so!* Surely you corrected the story?'

He shrugged. 'Aw, they had to boost morale, somehow, give folk something to think about besides losing the war — '

'But Dean got the medal for being a 'hero' for something that never happened!'

'It didn't worry me: he could have the medals. I was just glad the damned livin' hell was finally over.'

Beth was looking at him closely now. 'And Dean's climbed to success — even *riches* on false glory.'

She waited for his reply but he just stared back, in silence.

'Has — has he been worried because you know the truth, and you could ruin him if you wanted to? Was *that* the basis of your falling-out?'

'Aw, I doubt if it would matter now; too late to prove anything even if I wanted to. I guess it could be in the back of Dean's head. He's that sort of man, ambitious, remembers those things. Mebbe he's afraid that some time, when I'm really pissed at him — oops! Sorry, didn't mean to say that . . . '

'No need to apologize, I'd be *pissed* at him, too.'

He smiled. 'Nice to know someone agrees with me.'

'It must be a worry for you, though, Matt. It's not a light thing if you give it some thought.'

'Leaves a bad taste in my mouth sometimes,' he admitted, 'but, well, the medal and stuff gave Dean the push he needed and he's done well. We met up again when he was just on the rise and we did some contract trail-driving. Dean figured that beef would be in short supply just about everywhere, and he was right. We got plenty of work for a while . . . '

His voice trailed again and she asked, 'Why didn't it last?'

'Could've, but Dean had a bad habit of slapping our brand on anything with horns and four legs and selling it along with the contracted stuff as part of our private stock. I had no notion to see the inside of the State Pen, and we split up. I think we might still be wanted in some parts of Texas for cattle stealing, matter of fact.'

'But you're still friends?'

'Still . . . somethin'. A little less than friends. Not sworn enemies or anything. Dean went into other things, dabbled in buying land and stuff like that. I just drifted. Enjoyed seeing different places.'

'And ended up here,' she said. 'I can see why Dean might be a trifle edgy having you around while his career is on the rise again. He's quite rich now and playing with politics, I hear. But surely he wouldn't do anything extreme?'

'He's got nothin' to worry about: I'm not interested in knocking him off his pedestal. But — yeah, OK, he does have a long memory, and he's a lot more ruthless than he was.'

'And more powerful, Matt, if what I hear about him entering politics now that we're being considered for full statehood is true. Well, you shouldn't forget that.'

7

BUSHWHACKER

Matt Lacy had long ago developed a sixth sense for danger.

It had grown and strengthened over the war years, working behind Yankee lines, and, afterward, on the dodge from blood-crazed Indians, or murderous trail wolves willing to kill a man for a dime, and, once, a booze-sodden posse searching the Border for *Norteamericanos*, earning twenty *pesos* per dead man. Matt Lacy's senses had been tuned like a cat's, warning him even in his sleep when danger threatened.

It had paid off many times and now it had become a part of him — an *essential* part — there when it was needed.

Usually, there was no sudden alarm, just an uneasiness, sharpened nerves and vision, senses attuned more than usual to the actions of his mount . . . especially if it was in mountain-lion country, like here, below the so-called Drunken Forest. The land was rocky, the slopes scraggy with bushes that seemed to grow in just the right place to hide a waiting predator. The summer before he had gone to prison, Lacy recalled how, one blazing hot day, he couldn't figure out why his buckskin mount didn't want to pass through the shadow of a small bluff; it was late afternoon, when the shadows had thickened and stretched.

The horse snorted, tossed its head, making Matt rear up in the saddle, just in time to see the hurried passage of a man between two boulders. The sun glinted from the long rifle barrel as the man knelt and raised the gun to his shoulder.

Matt was already on his way out of the saddle, his Winchester sliding from the scabbard. It hung-up briefly — blade foresight catching in a raised double ridge of rough stitching, firm enough to jar Matt so that he fell forward over the horse's neck — which literally saved *his* neck.

He felt the airwhip of the bullet as it streaked past his ear and then he rolled away from the mount, working the rifle lever, saw the shooter in the rocks, standing now, so as to get a better sight on his target.

Instead of trying to stop his slide, Matt Lacy kicked into the ground, felt gravel cut through his shirt and tear at his shoulders as he was propelled backwards.

It threw the killer off, his next two rapid shots kicking dirt and stone beside Matt's sliding body.

The bushwhacker didn't get a third shot.

Matt, shoulders resting firmly against the cushion of dirt his slide had built up now, sighted, triggered, levered and triggered again, so fast the racket of the shots blended into a single roar.

The man up there went down on his

knees, both hands clawing into his chest, bright blood running between his fingers before he toppled on to his face and slid a few feet. The old training had come back with a vengeance and Matt Lacy was no longer visible. He was crouching on one knee behind a thick bush with grey-green leaves.

Five full minutes later he was still in the same spot, only his chest moving with his shallow breaths.

Then he edged carefully across the slope, keeping as much cover as he could between himself and the bush-whacker.

A few seconds later he was kneeling beside the fatally wounded man, holding the cocked rifle with one hand, while he slid the other inside the shirt, grimacing as he felt the hot, pulsing blood. It stopped almost immediately, became no more than a sluggish ooze when the killer's heart stilled forever.

He had seen this man before, riding with Dean Lewis's group, a couple of times. Later, the same man had been in a fight in the saloon and it had taken the sheriff and two townsmen a whole lot of grunting and cussing before they broke it up.

As they staggered apart, this man who now lay dead at Matt Lacy's feet, had snarled at his victim:

'Buy a mirror so you can see behind you, McGill! One time I'll be there and you'll be dead!'

He was still yelling threats as they dragged him away and threw him in the cells.

'Bad sonuver, that one,' one of the watching men said in a hoarse whisper. 'They say he used to make a livin' as a bounty hunter, an' if he couldn't find the wanted man, then he'd shoot anyone and fix him up with papers and such that said he was the man on the dodger so he could collect the bounty.'

And now that same man had just tried to kill Matt Lacy — here on his own range — or what he hoped *would* be his home range once he proved-up. *One of Dean's riders....*

Dean had said the man was a drifter, worked for him occasionally when he needed a stake. 'Calls himself *Foot* — short for *Footloose*. Cocky sonuver.'

Dean had made a joke out of it but Matt was uneasy just the same: he could think of no reason why Foot would want to kill him unless someone paid him to try.

It hadn't made him feel any easier when the dead man's paint horse trotted out of the brush, whinnied, and was answered by Matt's mount. The paint came down, obviously seeking company. It was still ten feet away when Matt's sharp gaze saw the dusty brand on its flank:

D Bar L. So this bushwhacker still had definite — and clear — connections with Dean Lewis.

*   *   *

That seemed like a long time ago, but suddenly Matt Lacy had that same strange feeling of disquiet as he mounted, a hand on his rifle, and looked around in time to see a rider charging out of the brush. He held a rifle out to one side as his horse came sliding and snorting down the slope, heading straight for Matt.

Matt wrenched the sorrel's head around and pulled the horse by main force on to a narrow strip of ground. As the other mount raced by, now just below him, Matt drove his heels violently into the sorrel's flank.

It gave a brief snort and instinctively jumped forward. It sailed clear across the other horse, knocking the panicked rider out of the saddle. Matt had his hands full keeping his mount on its feet as it slid and stumbled, the rider it had knocked off the other horse rolling, spinning and sliding down-slope.

He stopped with his boots resting against a shale boulder and lay there, dazed, bleeding a little from one nostril.

On foot, Matt struggled across the few yards of steep slope and launched himself at the other rider who was now swaying, blinking, and stumbling like a drunk. Matt reached out, caught a handful of dusty clothing and heaved back. The man grunted as he fell against a boulder, his flat-crowned grey hat knocked cockeyed to hang by the chin strap down one side of his neck. Blood trickled across his face now, a little dripping from his chin.

It was Jake Fargo, dazed, bruised and looking mighty sorry for himself.

'Out of luck again, Jake,' Matt said slowly, rifle covering the battered man. 'The stampede didn't get me, now you've botched your bushwhack. I take it you're not stupid enough to want to try again?'

Jake blinked and shook his head. It was then that Matt saw his face fully: bruised, swollen along one jaw, a deep cut above the right eye, upper lip split, a tooth missing.

'You been in a fight?'

Jake, a mid-sized man, looked mighty sad as he half-closed his eyes and moved his head in a slow negative. 'Wouldn't call it a fight — Bronco beat me up.'

Matt's face showed nothing of the surprise he felt. Before he could ask why, Fargo said in a low voice that sounded as much ashamed as it did worried, '*He* told me to . . . kill you and make it look like an accident that time with the cows.'

'By stampeding them in my direction, huh? Folk'd figure it was just my bad luck, bein' in the wrong place at the wrong time, as they took me over the cliff with them.'

Jake nodded miserably. 'You were too damn quick!'

'You were quick enough to try again — like now.'

'Aw — look, OK, I guess I've killed once or twice before, but . . . only when I had to . . . I never liked it.'

'*Had* to?'

Jake nodded slowly. 'When I was told to. I know I'm dumb! Only things I savvy is 'punchin' an' . . . how to shoot.

I'm no good at anythin' more compli-
cated.' His voice dropped to a whisper.
'I — I cain't even write my own name!'

Matt felt a twinge of pity for this
rough, uneducated cowpuncher trying
to make a living the best way he knew
how. *There were plenty like him
roaming the West.*

'Jake,' — Matt handed him three
silver dollars he took from his pocket
— 'all I have 'til payday. A mite less
than what you hoped for, I guess.'

'Damn! I'll say! This won't take me
far!'

'Well, it's yours, however little.
Bronco won't be happy you messed-up
again. I was you, I wouldn't go back to
D Bar L, I'd just keep riding.'

Jake tensed as Matt eased his rifle
across his legs, and looked carefully
around the slope, as if he half expected
the brutal ramrod to appear. 'I don't
take well to any man beatin' me, but
that Bronco scares me! He gets within
reach of me again, he'll kick me to
death!'

'I could save Bronco the trouble just by squeezing this trigger.'

Fargo straightened quickly, wincing as the movement caused him a stab of pain. 'No, that ain't your style. I seen you couple times when you was deputy marshal in Tucson, and again in Nogales, when you nailed some bloody-handed 'breed. You banged him up some and threw him in jail and brung him to trial, legal-like. Recall the smart-mouth lawyer diggin' at you 'cause you had a rep as a fast gun: 'Why didn't you save the county some money, Mr Lacy, and, er, execute the prisoner as usual?' An' you told him, 'Didn't want to do you out of a legal fee, Counsellor'. Which he did *not* like a whole helluva lot, an' you said: 'Oh, he's a miserable son of a bitch, all right, Counsellor, but there's a man out back right now, waitin' to be called to the stand: swears he saw this feller lyin' dead drunk, unable to move, way across in Oberon at the very time someone said Miss Phelan was being abused and killed'.' Fargo grinned. 'You had an argument with him, but he had to listen to the evidence of the other feller, who was a sawbones' helper an' had some standin' in the community. They got that 'breed on somethin' else later, as I recall, but he escaped, an' you chased him down and shot him in a gunfight.'

'Right, Jake, but what am I gonna do with you? You don't wanna go back to Dean or Bronco or ride out. Mmmm — mebbe I could take you in to Sheriff Quinn?'

Fargo scoffed. 'Might's well shoot me here and now.'

'How's that?'

'Aw, you mightn't know it, but most folk do: Dean Lewis pays for Marko Quinn's boy to go to college in Denver.'

After a moment, Matt Lacy said, 'Likes to play with loaded dice, old Dean, don't he? Well, I think it's time you found yourself a new job, Jake. Say somewhere in Cheyenne — a long ways from here, anyway. Because next time I

131

see you, I'll shoot to kill. What d'you say?'

Jake Fargo ran a tongue across his split lips, blinked again, then nodded jerkily. 'I — I think I'm halfway there already!'

'You're smarter than I reckoned.'

'Er — only thing is — I ain't been paid this month an' I won't be now, that's for sure.' He jingled the three coins. '*They need a lotta company!*'

Matt pursed his lips briefly, suddenly lifted his rifle and fired past Jake Fargo's head, the man yelling in alarm and ducking. Matt said, pointing, 'See that white mark on the skinny cottonwood where I just shot off a piece of bark? 'Bout a man's height up the trunk?'

'Y — yeah.' Fargo's voice was not too steady. 'What about it? It's a long shot, but nothin' special. I could likely hit that tree from here.'

'No, Jake, I don't want you to potshot it, I want you to *ride* for it. If you can reach it before I'm ready to shoot again, you get to keep on going.' His voice changed and he levered another cartridge into the Winchester's breech, the metallic clash sounding very loud. Blood drained from Fargo's dirt-smeared face. 'Want to give it a try?'

'Aw, now listen. I — It weren't my idea to try to kill you!'

'But you're the one did try.'

'I — I *had* to! Judas, Bronco'll blame me for lousin'-up again, not finishin' the job on you! Look, gimme a break, Lacy! I want to get the hell outa here, but I'm bust! I tell you — I need money, man!'

'Hey, Jake, I'm giving you something better than money, you damn fool! I'm giving you your *life*! You make it to that tree I marked and you can keep on ridin' up and over the crest of the range. Where you go then is up to you, but you need to start — *now*!'

Fargo only hesitated briefly, made ready to spur his mount away, but looked down at Matt one more time.

'I sure wish I had me some real *dinero*. But, I — well, here's somethin' — three dollars' worth!' He widened an already crooked smile. 'It ain't that land Dean's interested in so much, though it's part of it, it's the river!'

'The river? He's already got the deep bend on his land and more'n enough water for his cows. And it ain't *my* river.'

'No, I savvy you cain't never have that land, bein' an ex-con, but he's afraid you might start the Law lookin' into just how he got that prove-up land transferred to his name. It was s'posed to go back into what they call 'The Pot' — *Land Retrieval*, it means, for a re-draw, when you went to jail. Give someone else a chance at it, you know? I dunno the details but Dean an' that land agent, Zac Heffner, worked somethin' between 'em so's Dean could get what used to be your land, and it cain't be legal because he's too blamed rich to qualify for a gov'ment grant!'

And that's why Dean'd rather see me dead than let me run around asking questions, Matt thought.

'You're holding back, Jake, ain't you? There's something else — about the river.'

Jake looked less than eager, fighting some hard decision. Then: 'Ah, what the hell? I reckon what I'm gonna tell you is worth a *thousand* bucks, but . . . ' He shrugged, sighing. 'OK, I might's well tell you.'

Matt just looked at him steadily.

Fargo sighed again, sat straighter in the saddle as he said, 'Well, for whatever it's worth, he's aimin' to bring in paddle-wheelers.'

Matt frowned. 'Paddle-wh — ?'

Fargo looked scared now: he'd said too much and couldn't go back. He swallowed, tried to spit but his mouth was too dry. He said with a rush of words, 'For shipping his steers!'

Matt got it then. Of course! Move the beef to market by river, save all the trouble and expense of a trail drive, get to the buyers weeks ahead of the dust-eaters.

'He'll make a goddamn fortune!' Fargo said bitterly and threw Matt a mock salute, ready to run his mount for the timber. 'But you or me won't see one red cent of it!'

'You're still breathin' and able to ride, Jake. Count your luck. Now, get movin'! I'm ridin' nighthawk tonight and I need to get some shut-eye. *Adios.*'

He raised the rifle and Jake found enough courage to scowl and mutter a curse before he spurred away.

Well, Matt thought, watching him go, whatever else he might be, Dean Lewis was mighty slick when it came to making — or saving — a dollar.

Whatever it might cost to do so.

8

NIGHTHAWK

Beth — and her crew — were surprised when Matt told them about the attempt on his life by Jake Fargo.

'I'm not sure he was really trying, but then again, he was scared white every time Bronco Cutler's name was mentioned.'

'Be a good amount of luck in it, either way,' opined Lofty, unsmiling. 'For you.'

Matt gave the short cowboy a steady look, nodded gently. 'A lot of luck. Fargo was a mess, thanks to Bronco. Likely overdid it, shook him up so much he couldn't hit the side of a barn with a shotgun. Otherwise I mightn't be here now.'

'But he made his try?'

Matt nodded at Beth with a suggestion of a smile. 'He did. But he failed, so now he's hitting the high slopes and is likely to finish up a long way from Buckshot Ridge . . . somewhere Bronco can't reach him.'

Beth passed the potatoes to the cowboy on her left but remained looking at Matt Lacy. 'If Bronco Cutler ordered Jake — or whoever else — to try to kill you, who ordered Bronco in the first place?'

'It has to be Dean.'

'But why would he want to kill you? *Now*, I mean. If he wanted you dead, there have been so-so many times when it could've happened.'

Matt pursed his lips. 'You ask good questions, Beth, better than the answers I can give.'

'It's just that I had the impression that while there's some sort of animosity between you, it wasn't anywhere near outright hatred.'

Matt Lacy shrugged and used a small piece of cornpone to mop up the gravy remaining on his plate. He put it into his mouth and spoke around it.

'Me neither, but Dean's a man of many moods. Some things that rile him one time don't even bother him enough to miss a draw on his cigarette another. There's something in the wind, all right. Maybe something to do with his playing with politics. With Dean, it's likely more than a game, but — I really have no idea what's happening.'

'Me, I wouldn't need to know the reason someone wanted to kill me, I'd git. Or, if I was stupid enough, mebbe go lookin' for him.' That was the dour Montana.

Matt smiled crookedly. 'Funny you should say that . . . '

'You're not serious!' Beth was clearly shocked. 'I mean, the man's intentions are very clear now. If you go hunting Bronco he'll be just waiting to finish the job!'

'You're likely right, Beth.' Matt stood, pushing his chair back to the table. He paused, looked straight into her face and said, 'I dunno any other way, but I'll do my stint of nighthawkin' before I make up my mind for sure.'

'Hell, you be careful, Matt! I — I could split it with you, if you want . . . ?'

Matt shook his head at Cleve Baxter. 'Thanks, anyway, Cleve, but I reckon I can handle it.'

'Matt, Cleve's right. It's too dangerous now there have been actual attempts on your life — and it'll be dark.'

He was already at the door of the big kitchen, paused with his hand on the latch.

'Makes me a harder target,' he said, going out into the night.

But he was more cautious as he approached the slope where he knew the early nighthawk would be watching the herd.

'Time to go in and enjoy that steak Beth's cooked for your supper, Danny. Don't let it get cold.'

'Thanks for bein' on time, Matt.' Danny hauled rein almost alongside Matt's sorrel. 'Dunno if it means anythin', but there's some kinda animal, I guess.' He gestured vaguely. 'On that slope, in the brush, some-wheres. Must be caught up. Makin' a kinda whimperin' sound. Don't think it's dangerous, but you never know. Likely one of them white-wolf pups. It's whelpin' time for 'em, so watch out for Momma Wolf if you go take a look.'

'Thanks, Danny, I'll be careful.'

Danny spurred away, belly growling at the thought of hot food, and Matt dismounted and sat down amongst some rocks while he rolled and lighted a cigarette. The small herd was settling in, even though it was still early, with just a single bright pink-and-yellow line in the sky above the hills. He smoked with the cigarette's glowing end cupped in his hand and was exhaling when he paused, allowing the smoke to trickle back over his lips. Then —

He heard something and thought it must be the trapped animal Danny had mentioned — must have a foot caught or something. It was making a kind of half-moan, half-growl. He didn't care for any creature to be suffering, stood slowly, pinching out the cigarette, putting the butt in his shirt pocket for later. Easing the sixgun in its holster, he paused, holding his breath to cut down extraneous noise, and listened again.

He nodded: the poor beast was in pain, all right. He didn't know what it might be but it sure wasn't one of the cows: it would be bellowing its head off. He held the gun with thumb on the hammer spur just in case whatever it might be was ready to snap and snarl and bite at anything within reach if the pain was really hurting now.

When he first saw the vague outline he stopped in his tracks, bringing up the gun as he felt sweat prickle the back of his neck.

The hell was it . . . ? Looked big enough to be a —

'Judas Priest! It *is* a man!' Not so big, but a *man*.

He knelt swiftly, eyes a little more used to the darkness now, but night was solidifying fast and blackness closed around him. His probing left hand felt a hairy chest heaving spasmodically in a rumpled, torn shirt, harsh air hissing through a half-closed throat.

'Who are you, feller?' Matt asked hoarsely, and wasn't prepared for the answer.

It was a kind of coughing, part-grunt, part-gurgling, but he could make out the word: '*F-Far-go* . . . '

'Jesus, Jake! What the hell happened? You been shot? Take a tumble from your hoss?'

'Bron-co . . . '

Matt tensed. 'You saying Bronco Cutler did this to you?' He felt the head move in a nod. 'Dammit, Jake, I thought you weren't going back to D Bar L!'

'H — had to. Needed a get-away . . . stake.'

'You told me you never had any money — hadn' been paid.'

'S — s'right. B — but had — ' The rasping voice went silent for so long, Matt thought he had died, but then Jake said, quite strongly and clearly,

'H-had somethin' I found in Dean's room a while back. Figured it was worth a bit an' I could sell it for a stake.'

He paused and Matt started to ask what he had been doing in Dean's room, but decided it was irrelevant right now. 'You get whatever it was?'

The sweaty head moved slowly in a slow nod. 'In m — my p — pocket. Was gonna — sell it. My *left pocket*.'

Matt's groping fingers found the object: it felt kind of rough, metallic, and there were — well, they felt like small buttons here and there. He pulled it free and it lay across his hand, protruding both sides, which made it four or five inches long, but he could tell nothing by feel in the dark, although — He caught his breath as he suddenly thought he *did* recognize it, when Jake gasped, 'It's the one . . . Tommy McDermott tried to kill you . . . with in that fight . . . '

Yes! That's what it was: the deadly little knife McDermott had pulled from his boot-top, the sheath coming with it and falling off the blade, razor-honed.

The knife Dean Lewis swore McDermott had never had! But he must have found it later and taken it away to his room and hid it, likely because it looked valuable.

'It's gotta be worth s — somethin',' gasped Jake Fargo. 'Gold — filigree, studded with — with jewels — '

He made some terrible noises then and Matt thought Jake was dying, but the man rallied after a brief bout of bubbling coughing. 'Aw — *Christ!* Them boots of Bronco's m-must be — be red with my blood! Ribs're . . . mush — '

'Better not talk, Jake. I'll get one of Beth's men to fetch the sawbones.'

'Too late for that. Br-Bronco shot me, too — under left shoulder. D-dumped me . . . here. A warnin', I . . . g — guess I'm thr — through, M — Matt, all thr — *Aw, God!*'

Jake Fargo paused, his breath harsh and rattling in the back of his throat.

Matt saw the man's eyes fly wide and then there was a hand grabbing wildly at him, surprisingly strong, as Jake flailed in sudden, mindless convulsions, while the terrible pain clawed at his insides.

He screamed, making Matt stagger back, lose balance and half-sprawl awkwardly. Then, with some massive, writhing effort, he half-rose with a final surge of pain-driven energy, and either fell or flung himself at the scrambling Lacy, knocking him over completely.

Matt instinctively fought off the flailing hands but fell with the dying Fargo on top of him, still punching and eye-gouging wildly, the force of the blows weakening swiftly.

Matt tried to squirm out from under but their legs had become entwined and he grunted with effort, sure now that Jake was already dead.

Dead, maybe, but not about to lie down.

Then Matt did a little panicking of his own: Jake, muttering gibberish, was scrabbling at Matt's sixgun, now hanging half out of its holster. With a mighty effort he bucked and squirmed and kicked until Jake fell away, but the Colt went with him, and, even as Fargo finally died, his fingers closed convulsively and triggered a wild shot.

Matt found himself with a mouthful of dust and his face half buried in more, where he had slammed flat at the instant the gun fired.

But it was all over now. Jake Fargo sprawled unmoving across his legs, contorted face staring up at the stars, the smoking gun lying in the dirt a yard away.

'Matt! *Matt!* You OK?'

It was Danny's voice; he rode up the slope, early for Matt's relief, and: 'What're you doin' back here? Cleve's s'posed to relieve me.'

'Aw, guess I'm a mite curious about that trapped animal. Was wonderin' if mebbe it was a man?'

Panting, swallowing to get enough breath, Matt called, 'You were wrong about the white wolf cub — turned out to be Jake Fargo. He's dead now. You better have Beth send for the sheriff. I'll wait here.'

There was a brief silence. Then Danny said, as he turned his horse downslope again, his voice drifting up through the darkness, 'Yeah, I'll go back right away. But — why'd you shoot him, Matt?'

Matt was too stunned to answer at first and the kid's horse was moving away when he finally jumped up, calling, 'I never shot him, kid! Christ, he grabbed the gun and it just went off . . . he was wild, and I mean *wild*!'

He let his voice drift off as Danny disappeared into the night.

'God-*damn*! I hope he don't go spreading that kinda talk!' Matt said aloud.

'Why not? It's the truth, ain't it?' asked a deep voice that brought Matt around in a crouch, fumbling for the gun that was no longer in his holster. 'Aw, now, ain't that a pity you ain't wearin' a gun, Lacy. Guess we'll just have to keep you covered till the kid gets back with the sheriff.'

'The hell're you doing here, Bronco?'

Cutler laughed briefly. 'Came lookin' for poor ol' Fargo. Thought I'd finished him, but I just had to come see how long he was gonna last.'

'OK,' Matt said tightly. 'Let's just sit and wait for the sheriff. I think he'll be interested in what Jake told me before he died.'

'Well, let's just wait an' see, huh? Now don't go gettin' notions of makin' a run for it. Kinda forgot to tell you, I got a couple sidekicks upslope a'ways.' He raised his voice a little. 'You hear me, Slim — Keno?'

'Hear you, Bronco. You want us down there?' a voice called out of the darkness.

'Yeah, better if you come. Whaddaya say, Lacy?'

Matt had nothing at all to say, simply raised his hands at Bronco Cutler's command.

He sat down on a rock and, under the close scrutiny and guns of the three D Bar L riders, carefully took the skeen-do from his pocket and concentrated on examining it.

Dean Lewis had kept quiet about this very knife at Matt's trial. If he had spoken up and handed it over, it would have given Matt a chance at a verdict of self-defence and maybe only a token sentence — or even none at all.

'Instead, I got three years of *hell*! While this damn knife lay somewhere in Dean Lewis's room gathering dust!'

Under the guns of Dean's men, Matt examined the knife again in the pale light, the edge of a waxing moon just showing at the third peak of the hills. He turned it this way and that, felt the long-dormant rage rising within, almost choking him.

As his hand closed over the knife, he said through clenched teeth: 'Somebody's gonna wish they'd never been born!'

'Well, his name just might be

Matthew Lacy, you know that?' The two D Bar L cowhands laughed as Bronco grabbed the knife, glanced at it briefly and shoved it into a pocket.

Then the big ramrod brought up his gun and laid the barrel across the side of Matt's head, knocking his hat off. He hit him again for good measure and Matt fell like a pole-axed steer in the slaughterhouse.

9

CALL IN THE LAW!

It was closer to three hours than two before Sheriff Marko Quinn arrived.

And he was not in a happy mood.

'You goddamn range rannies!' he growled crabbily as he dismounted stiffly. 'Think nothin' of disturbin' a man at his own business.' His voice changed to falsetto: '*Oh, Sheriff! — Sheriff! — You busy, Sheriff? Just got a leetle trouble you might like to look into. Oh, where? Well, not right handy, but only about ten, mebbe twelve miles out. You know, Flyin' C? Beth Casey's place. Hope we ain't disturbin' you, Sheriffff!*'

Then his voice returned to normal, edged with barely contained anger. ''Course you're not disturbin' me, boys! Why I'm proud to make myself

152

available to help you out. Now! What the goddamned hell is it you've drug me all this way for?'

Bronco Cutler, unfazed by the lawman's bitter words, nodded to his men and they dragged the semiconscious Lacy across, his boot toes trailing twin marks in the dust. They'd made a camp-fire while awaiting Marko's arrival and he took a cup of coffee now and sipped as they dumped Matt before him. The sheriff nudged him roughly with a boot.

'Where's the kid Lacy sent for you?'

'Home in bed, where *I* oughta be.' He nudged the unconscious Lacy again. 'The hell's he been up to?'

'Oh, nothin' much,' Bronco told him. 'Just beat the hell outa poor Jake Fargo, then shot him for good measure. Lucky we heard the shot or he mighta got away.'

'So you jumped him? Caught him redhanded, like?'

'Not quite, but, yeah we jumped the son of a bitch and I laid him out with

153

my gun barrel when we seen what he'd done to Jake.'

Bronco, big and tall as he was, reared back, looking alarmed in the glow of the fire as Marko rounded on him with a savagery he'd never seen before in the lumbering lawman.

'*Then why the blue-damned hell didn't you drag him into town instead of makin' me haul-ass all the way out here!*'

Bronco glared back. ''Cause — 'cause we figured you bein' the Law, you'd want to see Jake where we found him!'

'The hell for? I know what a dead man looks like: shot, beat-up, dragged behind a hoss, whatever. You coulda brought Jake in to me!'

'Judas, Marko, you can be a cantankerous son of a bitch at times!'

'You just watch out this ain't one of them, Bronco!' The lawman turned to the silent Lacy, blood sticky on his face where it had run down from the gunwhipping. 'You got anythin' to say?'

'I never touched Jake. Found him near-dead, already beat-up and shot in the back. He said Bronco done it.'

'The *back*! Now there's a nice touch! Short-assed feller like Jake Fargo, wouldn't come to your shoulder and someone has to shoot him *in the back*!'

'Well, don't look at me!' Matt slurred and jerked his head in Bronco's direction. 'He's the one you want.'

'Aaaah!' growled Bronco Cutler, stepping forward and driving a fist into Matt's midriff. Lacy gagged and dropped to his knees, head hanging as he fought for air. 'He's lyin' in his teeth, Marko. Ask the boys here: we heard the shot an' come a'runnin' and this scum was bendin' over what was left of poor Jake.'

Of course the cowboys backed Bronco's story.

Sheriff Quinn was silent for a short time, then brought out a set of manacles. 'Hold him. Hands in front!'

Matt struggled but knew it was futile — and in less than two minutes he was cuffed, his hands already going numb, the iron rings were clipped so tightly.

'Get him on a hoss and follow me into town. With a little luck I *might* manage to grab me a couple hours' shuteye before sun-up.'

He punched Matt in the back, sending him staggering.

'Damn you!' Then plodded to his horse, mounted and rode off into the darkness.

'Judas! He musta missed out on somethin' at home, huh?' opined one of Bronco's sidekicks.

The other one shook his head. 'Nah. Think it's the new gal he's got — that widder-woman who moved into the dressmaker's place, right next to the law office. Chuck Downey reckons she never even closes the blinds in the fittin' rooms. Musta got old Marko there feelin' randy.'

All three laughed. Matt Lacy didn't seem to think there was anything funny about it. Somewhere close by a coyote howled mournfully.

Mebbe it was about the best farewell poor Jake Fargo could expect: he lay, almost unnoticed, half-under a grubby blanket.

* * *

'Don't lock that door!'

The sheriff, busy fitting a large key into the square lock on the cell door, looked up sharply. He scowled at the dishevelled Matt Lacy on the other side of the bars.

'Oh? You like it better if I left it open?'

'Don't have to be open ... just unlocked.'

'Oh, is that all?' The lawman snorted and turned the key. The lock made a kind of clashing sound. 'Sure, I leave it unlocked and in the mornin' I find it wide open and you nowhere to be seen. I din' think even you was that dumb, mister!'

'I spent three damn years bein' locked-up each night and sometimes most of the day. Wasn't always a cell, neither. They had *boxes* there specially made for the prisoners. They'd cram us in, nail the lids down while we was all scrunched up — only opened 'em up when they felt like it. I don't care for enclosed places, Sheriff, not so bad if I knew the doors ain't locked, but — '

'This ain't no hotel, you murderin' son of a bitch. You'll stay here, *door locked*, as long as I say. Now shut up an' lemme get some shuteye.'

'Aw, come *on*! You don't need to do this, Marko! I never killed Jake Fargo and — '

'*Shut the hell up!* Now you disturb my sleep and I swear you'll wish you was back in one of them boxes you just mentioned! Savvy?'

Matt didn't bother answering but he felt the sweat starting to ooze from his pores as if someone had turned on a tap. His stomach was already knotting-up: he had fought this for a long time, but had never really got over being locked in — as against locked up.

Especially that time when the mad Mexican had set the prison block on fire....

Eleven men had died that night because their doors were *locked* and the heat of the flames had made it impossible to unlock them. He had been the only survivor in his part of the cell block.

* * *

Sheriff Marko Quinn was sleeping peacefully, nothing on his conscience to keep him awake. He was in the large, soft bed of Adeline Hislop, the town's new dressmaker, and she lay next to him, warm against his back.

'Marko, Marko, *Marko*!'

She almost shouted this last and rammed an elbow into his ribs, bringing him awake, cursing.

'Judas Priest! Wh-what the hell's wrong?' He felt her then and moaned. 'Look, I ain't ready for more lovin' yet, sweetie. Gimme another hour, huh?'

'I'll give you about three minutes!'

'You crazy . . . ? Jesus! Watch them elbows, will ya!'

'Listen, you damn fool. *Listen*!'

Blinking sleep from his eyes, the sheriff sat up and pulled faces as he tried to convince her he *was* listening — for what, he didn't know.

And then: 'Aw, shoot! That damn drifter in his cell! He's gone loco!'

'Yes! And he's been shouting and rattling the bars or something for over an hour while you've been — '

'Aw, he's got some sorta problem about his cell door bein' locked. Yeah, yeah, I know: it *has* to be locked but he reckons he can't sleep if it is and — '

'You get over there right now!'

'What?'

'Right now, I said! And you quiet him down, or don't bother coming back here expecting to get into *this* bed — ever again!' She flung herself away from him and punched a pillow. '*I need sleep*. And I better get it right soon. Well, what're you waiting for?'

Marko groaned and rolled out of bed, hopped about looking for his clothes and cussed and stumbled around while he got dressed. 'By God, you better have somethin' special waitin' for me when I get back!'

'You've gotta go before you can get *back*!'

It was only when Marko found his way downstairs and groped his way to the front door of the dressmaking store that he realized he hadn't put on his boots.

But, yelping and jumping he somehow tippytoed his way next door to the law office and was in a right old mood by the time he crashed back the door of the cellblock. Matt had been yelling all the time and stopped now when the lawman appeared holding a hardwood club he'd taken from a desk drawer on the way in.

'You shut up that racket, you murderin' sonuver!' Marko swiped with the club, just missing Matt's fingers where they gripped the bars. 'You shut up or, I swear to God, I'll go get my Greener and give you both barrels through the bars!'

Matt looked wild, eyes staring, sheened with sweat, his clothes torn. He staggered to the bars, and shook the door. 'Come on, Marko!' he pleaded. 'Please! Just unlock the damn door!'

'I'll unlock your goddam brain if you've got one.'

Marko swiped at his fingers on the bars again and Matt stumbled back a couple of feet, hands out in an imploring attitude.

'You — you dunno what it's like.' Then he began shouting suddenly, just yelling without making any sense, an incoherent babble on a rising note, echoing off the hard cell walls.

Marko swore, unlocked the door and rushed into the cell, club raised, ready to crack Matt's skull.

But Matt ducked and propelled himself from the bunk, driving his head into Marko's midriff. The sheriff staggered against the bars, gasping, tried to lift the club for a strike. Matt grabbed the arm and twisted savagely and, suddenly, *he* held the club.

He bounced it twice off Marko's head — hard, hurting blows, a release for his frustrations, driving the sheriff to his knees where he made a grunting noise as he fell on his bloody face to the stone floor. Matt swiftly bent over him, taking the cell keys, stepped into the passage and locked the door — from the outside.

He tossed the keys way down the corridor and went into the front office.

It was maybe fifteen minutes before he left town, riding his sorrel which had been housed in the stables behind the jail, now with a sixgun and rifle taken from the law office.

The town was in near total darkness, murmuring with muted night sounds, except for the two saloons. *They* were making their usual racket of loud music, loud voices and an occasional fight.

If Matt Lacy was seen leaving town

by the dark back streets, no one tried to stop him.

Just as well because he was in a fighting mood.

10

FUGITIVE

There was only one place to go, of course, even though he didn't like involving Beth Casey any more than she already was.

Marko Quinn would be ready to chew nails and spit them out all bent and mangled when he came to — though Matt hoped the headache he was bound to have might slow him down some.

But he had little choice in his destination: he didn't yet know this country well enough to dodge a posse made up of locals — which it would be — so he needed help.

And the only person he could turn to was Beth Casey.

As the night breeze of his passage chilled the sweat on his face and body, he began to worry about that damned sheriff. *Had he hit him too hard?* Hell, he'd been mad enough to deliver fatal blows, but hoped he had retained enough good sense to just knock him out temporarily.

Ah, Marko was hard-headed: he had a reputation for being a brawling-type of lawman: he might start with his fists or his favoured club, but he wouldn't hesitate to resort to his guns if he figured he wasn't making enough of an impression.

Still, it would not be a good thing if old Marko upped and died.

'Hell! Don't even *think* that!' he murmured as he cleared the north edge of town, swung into the brush country in the opposite direction to Beth's Flying C. It wouldn't fool any good tracker for long, but if it delayed pursuit just a little . . . well, it had to be a plus.

The sorrel carried him on into the night.

* * *

She was waiting for him.

He didn't know what time it was — *hell, did it matter?*

Such thoughts only helped confuse things, bring uncertainty when clear decisions were needed, like *now*.

Somehow he found his way out of the dense brush, took a quick sight on the stars by giving the horse a blow at a small stream, then swung to his left.

He rode for maybe a mile before plunging into another stream, riding against the current until he could see the hill with its windmill that he knew was the southern boundary of Flying C.

Still he didn't make a direct approach, wound back into the brush, forced the less-than-happy sorrel through a thicket and came out behind the Flying C corrals. The restless mounts within the rails had sensed or heard the sorrel's approach and there was an exchange of whinnies and snorts as he made his way around towards the dark house.

'Bring your horse around the back of

the house, Matt!' called Beth in a low voice, but still startling him. 'I was hoping you'd come. This way. There's a lean-to here. I've already had a bag of grain and oats and so on put in. Leave your mount there. Danny'll take care of him. You come into the kitchen.'

He did as he was told, feeling a mite bewildered: he hadn't expected this. There was a sack of food and coffee on the table, a filled water canteen, even two boxes of cartridges for the Winchester.

She didn't light a lantern, worked by the glow from the cook fire, poured him coffee and took a plate of eggs and bacon from the warming shelf of the big kitchen range.

'Eat and drink. You can be on your way just as soon as you like. Here, I've drawn you a rough map you can use to get through the hills. There's a printed army map, too, you can take with you. It'll see you out of this country and across the State Line. Burn each map as you finish with it.'

'By God, Beth, you've gone to a helluva lot of trouble, for which I thank you. But you've also made a lot of trouble for yourself if they find out you helped me.'

'Burn the maps, like I said. There's nothing else that can be definitely traced back to Flying C. I've insisted the men stay put in their bunks. That way they aren't involved and they won't even have to lie when they say they haven't seen you.'

'Beth. I — I dunno what to say.'

'Stop talking and finish your coffee and begin eating. There should be enough to see you through till breakfast time which I hope will be a long way from here.'

He did as she ordered and she kept going to the windows, drawing the calico curtains aside. Without turning she said, 'Abe is up on the windmill. He'll strike a vesta if he sees anyone coming. You'll have plenty of warning.'

'Don't think I'm ever going to be able to repay you.'

'You don't have to, so forget it. *Forget it*, I said! More eggs? Bacon . . . ?'

'I'll take some of that cooked bacon. Can munch as I go. I — I feel like I'm running-out, leaving you to face Marko — and Dean.'

'There's nothing they can do to me,' she told him confidently, wrapping several strips of still-warm bacon in a square of cheesecloth.

'They'll know you helped me — won't have to *prove* it, they'll just *know*.'

'They'll *have* to prove any charges they make and it'll delay them and give you time to get clearer — ' Suddenly she looked at him sharply. 'You are clearing this neck of the woods, aren't you?'

He looked at her without speaking, chewing more food, and she sighed.

'Damn you, Matt Lacy. I knew it, I *knew* you wouldn't just go. You're knotheaded enough to merely hide out and — and *fight* powerful men like your so-called friend Dean Lewis. Oh, Matt, it's not worth it, whatever reason you may come up with.'

He paused in packing the cartons of cartridges into the small haversack she had provided.

'We used to be friends, Dean and me. We went through a lot together — a *helluva* lot. We had nothing, drifted from job to job, shared our last smoke, fought each other's battles and so on. I guess the damn war changed us.'

'It changed a lot of people, Matt.'

He nodded. 'Yeah, I s'pose we aren't the only ones to find out friendship don't always stand up to a heavy strain.'

'It must be a bitter pill for you to swallow, to know that a man you thought so much of has let you down so badly — even ordering you killed!'

'Hurts some,' he admitted in clipped tones, and began to gather his gear. 'I won't involve you further, Beth, you've already done too much. No, no, I mean if ever Dean finds out you helped me — well, maybe I can see that never happens.'

She glanced at him sharply, but didn't ask outright just what he meant by that last remark: Matt figured she was smart enough to figure it out.

'Will I ever see you again, Matt Lacy?'

He looked down into those blue eyes and forced a smile. 'You damn well better, but I'll choose *when*, that OK?'

On impulse, the point of her pink tongue running across her lips, she stepped forward, put both hands on his left arm and tugged until he tilted his head down.

She stood on tiptoe and kissed him on the mouth. '''Til then,' she said huskily.

He hesitated for only a few seconds, smiled and nodded. 'Be lookin' forward to it.'

Then he stepped out into the night where one of her men was waiting with the freshly rubbed-down sorrel. She watched him mount, but closed the door before he rode away.

She was surprised to see her hands were shaking.

She leaned her shoulders back against the door panels and took several deep breaths.

'Please — *please* just keep riding, Matt! I — I'll miss you terribly, but it'll be safer for you.

And harder for me! she told herself silently. *Oh a hell of a lot harder!*

⋆ ⋆ ⋆

He didn't get far.

He hadn't even cleared the Flying C boundary when he saw the man lying on the narrow walk-track that led to the windmill. He had swung a little too far west in the dark and hadn't meant to come over this way but now he was here . . .

He reined up, dismounted, sixgun in hand as he looked around carefully before approaching the prone figure. Even in the dark he recognized Abe Dulles's bow legs. Abe who had been keeping watch up on the windmill, according to Beth.

As he started to turn, there was a crackle of bushes behind him, but on the opposite side to the way he was turning.

Gun lifting, he whipped around, but something knocked his hat from his head and crashed against his skull, bright lights whirling in a brief Fourth-of-July.

Senses reeling, he was on his hands and knees and the night was a grey blur, seeming to alternately envelop him, then recede a little. That part was an illusion but the boot that drove into his side was real enough, and knocked him sprawling, gasping for breath.

Another boot stomped on his back and then a mocking voice he recognized even through the violent buzzing inside his skull, said, 'Figured you'd show up here sometime, Drifter! Now I've not only got you where I want you, but *her*, too! She helped a man wanted for murder. Be a pleasure watchin' the bitch try to wriggle outa that one.' There was a brief laugh. 'She'll find out this time I ain't *exaggeratin*'.'

So it was Milt Frazell, Matt thought, through the thudding inside his head. The man had hung around, waiting for an opportunity to get back at Beth for firing him and hiring Matt in his place.

'The hell d'you want, Milt?' Matt gasped as a boot pinned his head to the ground, the heel grinding, tearing flesh under his left ear and probably part of the ear itself.

'Nothin' much, just to square a few things and get myself in the good books of certain people.'

He let it hang in the air and Matt frowned. *It was almost as if he was waiting for Matt to ask 'Who . . . '*

So he asked, grinding out the word as his face was pushed harder into the ground.

Milt leaned over, rapped him — only lightly — with his gun barrel, but hard enough to send a lightning bolt of pain through Matt's neck.

'Oh, how about the new governor?' Frazell said, on a rising note. 'Reckon he might reward me if I hand him *you*?'

'Who the hell're you talkin' about? And get your damn boot off my head, will you?'

Milt's answer, of course, was to add more pressure.

'How's that?' chuckled Milt.

'No . . . damn . . . good!'

Matt gritted the words and during his writhing — only partly faked — got both hands pressed flat against the ground. He thrust up quickly — and violently.

Milt was still bending over him, gloating, and Matt's throbbing head drove into his grinning face with enough force to squash the man's nose: it made a squishy sound that was almost lost in a wild yell of intense pain. Milt fell, rolling on to his side, and Matt threw himself across his chest, groping for the man's gunhand.

He found it but was unable to get a good, firm grip and Milt Frazell triggered a wild shot that thundered into the night. Matt reared away, came back, still crouched, and drove an elbow across Milt's throat.

The big man gagged and rolled aside, kicking wildly. One of his boots glanced off Matt's forehead and he fell awkwardly. Milt, roaring in strangling pain, reared up and turned his gun on Matt.

There was another shot, but this time, Milt Frazell reared up, contorted face turning towards Abe Dulles who lay on his belly, his own smoking Colt held in both hands.

'Been wantin' to do that for a — a long time,' Abe Dulles gritted, even as Matt saw him fall forward, still holding his gun.

Milt Frazell was a huddled heap, eyes wide, blood trickling out of his slack mouth.

Somewhere, through the thundering pain in his head, Matt Lacy heard running feet and someone calling his name.

A woman's voice.

He was back in the Flying C kitchen.

Beth stood beside him, bathing his mangled earlobe with warm water and iodine. He writhed in the straightback chair, but gritted his teeth and tried not to groan too loud.

The other members of Beth's crew — except for Cleve — were outside, on watch. Milt's body was covered with a blanket, not yet buried. Abe had been treated for the large lump and cut on his head that Milt had given him when he jumped the man at the windmill. He was in the bunkhouse, sleeping now.

'Milt was always a vindictive man,' Beth said quietly as she dabbed some ointment on Matt's torn lobe, making him writhe. 'I just hope those gunshots don't bring in any of the D Bar L crew — the sound could carry to their south line.'

'They got no one workin' there, Beth,' said Cleve Baxter. 'Ain't started round-up in that section yet.'

She looked relieved. 'There. I'm sure that ear will still be painful but it's an awkward place to cover — unless you want a full head bandage?'

'No, that pad you've got on will be OK.' Matt had two more fairly deep cuts, one on the forehead, the other under the hair on top of his head. 'Don't suppose you'd have a slug of likker handy? Feel like I can do with one.'

'Er — we got a bottle in the bunkhouse,' Cleve said, looking at Beth warily. 'I know you told us not to keep likker there, Beth, but — '

'Go and fetch it, Cleve. I don't think I've got any in the house here.'

As the man left, Beth looked at the still slightly groggy Lacy. 'Are you sure you heard Milt right, Matt? He did say Governor?'

'That's what he said.'

'I haven't heard anything about the actual *appointment* of a governor, but he could mean Dean. *Would* mean him. We're being considered for state-hood now the big railroad linking us to

Santa Fe and Denver is near completion. We'd need a governor then, but how could someone like Milt believe he could be close to someone as high up as a governor?'

'Would he even *know* about something like that?' Matt countered. 'In the first place, I mean?'

'Oh, you don't — didn't — know Milt. He was a true busybody. Knew some very strange things and most times surprisingly accurately. He *worked* at gossip, tracked it down to its source many times. He thrived on that kind of thing. Made himself a lot of enemies, but it didn't seem to bother him.'

Cleve returned with the half-bottle of whiskey and Beth got glasses, surprising Matt by having a good-sized snifter of the liquor herself. Maybe she needed it: he sure did, and savoured the rawness as the drink went down.

'If Milt used his info right, he might've made himself some friends, too — or, leastways, people he could use to feed him the kinda stuff he wanted.'

She frowned. 'What're you saying? He blackmailed people who were in positions where they could get him certain information he could use for more blackmail?'

'If he was like you say.'

Beth frowned, said thoughtfully, 'Heavens! I — I didn't even consider that sort of thing! But it *is* possible.'

'I know he got hisself that big buckskin he rode by puttin' some sorta pressure on Ben Garson,' Cleve said.

At Matt's quizzical look, Beth said, 'Our biggest livery man.'

'Yeah,' agreed Cleve. 'Seems Ben had himself a little Mexican pretty stashed away somewhere. Milt found out about her and next thing he's forking one of the best hosses in the county.'

'Yes! We often wondered how he could afford that buckskin,' Beth said. 'I didn't know Milt had pressured Ben Garson.'

'So Milt *could* know something

about the appointment of a governor if he poked around enough — and in the right places,' said Matt, looking directly at the girl now. 'And Dean has been getting himself noticed lately: big rancher, having a say in the general running of the town, urging a town council be formed — and a war hero to boot.'

Beth drew in a sharp breath. 'You — you're thinking *Dean Lewis* really might be being considered?'

'He's got the right front for it. Which could also explain why he'd rather see me dead at this time.'

Beth was tense as she leaned forward a little.

'Because *you* know he never really earned that medal! You are the one person who can tell he wasn't as heroic as has been claimed and any such story — true or not — would ruin his chances of a governership, or anything else in the political line.'

'Distinct possibility, I reckon,' Matt agreed.

'Dean never even tried to correct that hero's picture of himself. He simply took the medal and all the glory that came with it. Rode on the back of false fame all these years and has probably been worrying most of that time that you might turn up sometime and expose him!'

'Well, it might've bothered him to a certain extent, I guess, but — and we're only surmising — if he *is* being considered as the first governor now, he'd want to make sure — *damned* sure — that I didn't do any talking out of turn at this point that'd stir things up.'

'That's why he's been trying to have you killed,' opined Cleve Baxter. He blew out his cheeks. 'Hey, I bet ol' Milt'd turn in his grave if he knew he's missin' out on all this. The kinda stuff he thrived on.'

'Providing we're on the right track,' Matt said quietly, drawing both their gazes. 'Yeah, I think we are, but — ah, to hell with it! It don't make sense any other way.'

Beth reached out and squeezed the surprised Lacy's hand. 'Well, at least now you *know* who your real enemy is.'

He nodded gently. 'Yeah.'

Cleve said slowly, 'All you gotta do is figure out what to do about it: a lone drifter agin a man powerful enough to be considered as the governor of the state!'

'I can't say I like the odds,' allowed Beth tautly.

She gave a little start of surprise as Matt turned to face her.

He was smiling.

11

THERE — AND BACK

Sheriff Marko Quinn wore a full bandage on his battered head, which throbbed and upset his vision at unexpected intervals. He had been violently ill twice and the doctor told him this was consistent with mild concussion.

'Whoever hit you stopped just short of killing you, Sheriff,' the sawbones told him.

'That was his mistake!' growled Quinn. 'The son of a bitch should've finished the job 'cause he's livin' on borrowed time now!'

'If you have any notions of chasing down this man,' the medic said in serious tones, 'I strictly advise against it. You need *rest*. And I mean *rest in bed*! Preferably alone. Any, *any* undue exertions could cause a brain haemorrhage, which, of course, would be fatal. No! You listen to me, for once, Marko! You ... take ... things ... *easy*! I won't be responsible otherwise.'

'I *know* who's *responsible* for the way I feel, Doc, and the son of a bitch is gonna learn he can't get away with it.'

'Man, are you deaf? I just told you how dangerous it is for you to get excited and — '

The lawman was on his feet, grabbed the edge of the battered desk to steady himself and made an obvious effort to square his shoulders.

'I heard you, Doc. Gimme a bottle of laudanum or somethin' if you wanta feel that you've done your job proper, but I'm going after my own medicine and, in case you're innerested, it's a mixture of red-eye an' gunpowder. You know what I mean?'

He strode to the door, fairly steadily, and as his hand closed on the knob, looked back at the angry medic.

'Relax, Doc. If I don't shoot straight,

186

I'll just be givin' you some extra custom. Can't complain about that, can you . . . ?' Halfway through the doorway he called back, 'Oh, just charge my visit to the county, OK?'

'Do you mean the cost of your funeral, too?'

Those words stopped Marko in his tracks, but only for a few seconds.

'I'll live to lay a wreath on your grave, you damn butcher!'

He slammed the door after him and, chest heaving now, leaned back against the wall.

Mebbe he was a mite too brash right now but, by God, he aimed to nail Matthew Lacy this time!

Nail him *dead!* No one — *no one* — beat his head in and figured to walk away afterward.

No — damn — way!

Then he whirled, grabbing quickly at the wall as the door was wrenched open behind him.

'Easy, Marko! Calm down, for heaven's sake! I almost forgot to mention, but you talking about funerals reminded me.'

The sheriff frowned. 'Yeah? What you on about, now, Doc?'

'A man was brought into me earlier — he'd been shot and he died. It was too late for me to do anything for him. So I passed his body along to my brother at his funeral parlour and — '

'That sounds about right if he was dead. You got a good thing goin' there, Doc, you and that brother of yours — you a sawbones and him a mortician. But, you ever gonna get to whatever you're tryin' to say?'

'Right! Here it is: the man was that hardcase Milt Frazell. I was told he was shot in a gun duel with another of Beth Casey's cowhands — Abe Dulles, who required my services for some head wounds . . . Not too serious, I'm glad to say.'

The lawman was alert now. 'This shootin' — took place out at Flyin' C?'

'So I am told. There was nothing I could do for Milt — ' But he was talking to the hot, humid air now.

The sheriff was hurrying towards the hitchrail where his horse was tethered and later the medico said he'd never seen Marko Quinn mount so quickly and quit town in such a hurry.

★ ★ ★

'You'd better come in and have a cup of coffee, Sheriff,' said Beth, as the sweating lawman climbed down from his lathered mount. 'You look rather pale.'

'Thanks to that friend of yours, Matt Lacy,' gasped Marko Quinn. 'I'll take that coffee, tho', Beth — and mebbe somethin' to give it a lift?'

She smiled. 'I think we can find something suitable.'

Once seated in the big ranch kitchen with his coffee laced generously with whiskey, the sheriff mellowed a little.

'Had some trouble out here, Doc tells me, a shootin'.'

'Well, it was some stupid argument

between a couple of my men that got out of hand. I was going to report it to you.'

'After you'd give Matt Lacy time to get away?'

She frowned. 'Matt Lacy hasn't been here.'

'Beth, don't gimme any stories! I had a look round before I rode in.'

'Yes, one of my men saw you. I'd rather you came straight to me if you want any particular information, Marko.'

He held up a big hand quickly. 'Don't try divertin' me, Beth. I found tracks left by that big sorrel Lacy rides — I know 'em well enough.'

'Well, they must be from the other day.'

He stood quickly, startling her. 'Beth! I ain't got time for this. One of your men is dead under suspicious circumstances and I know Lacy was here! He's wanted for attempted murder now — '

'Attempted — murder?'

He gave her a crooked, mirthless grin and jerked a thumb into his chest. 'Me! And I believe you've aided him to escape so I'm considerin' arrestin' you and takin' you to jail. You want to get your things?'

Beth was pale now: she hadn't expected *this*!

★ ★ ★

Dean Lewis looked up irritably from the letter he was writing at his desk as a servant showed Sheriff Quinn into his office. The lawman was quick to doff his hat as he saw the frown on Lewis's face.

'Sorry to interrupt, Dean.'

'*Mr Lewis*,' Dean snapped and Quinn swallowed.

'Sorry, I — '

'Will you quit being sorry every time you open your mouth and state your business. I'm a busy man.'

'I — I know, sir.' *That* ought to please him, Marko thought. 'It's just that I wanted to report on how things are goin' and — '

'Then *report*! And stop stammering.'

Marko swallowed again and hastily told the rancher about the trouble at Flying C, adding, 'I — er — I told Beth Casey I'd throw her in jail for helpin' Lacy 'cause he's officially a fugitive now.'

'In other words you have no idea where he is.'

'N-not right now, but I scared her some mentioning jail and I — well, I wanted to report to you and kinda get your opinion on that part.'

'Dammit, man! This is important, all right, but I don't want to be bothered with every small detail! *Do what you think is best*! If I think you need it, I'll back you up.'

'B — but, if I'm wrong . . . ? I mean, I just wanted to see if you approved . . . '

Dean's cold stare was positively frosty now. But he curbed his impatience and quickly gave some thought to what this fool was doing.

'Marko, you go ahead and put the Casey woman in jail. Just make sure you have a watertight reason for doing so. Put her — No! Let her stew a little with the *threat* of going to jail! Yes! That'll be better.'

Marko Quinn frowned. 'B — better, sir?'

'Decidedly so! You think Lacy is still hanging around Flying C?'

'Aw, he's somewheres out in that area, I'll bet my boots on that, but I also bet she's give him a map or told him the best places to hide out or the trails to take to the State Line.'

'Then it will need a posse to search for him?'

'Well that's another thing I was goin' to ask about.'

'Will it need a posse or not?'

Marko cleared his throat. 'I reckon so — '

'All right. Get some men and start your search, but make sure they do some shouting to each other about the possibility of the Casey woman going to jail.'

He paused to let that sink in and fought down his exasperation as Marko looked at him, obviously trying to savvy the rancher's reasoning.

'Just do exactly as I told you, Marko,' Dean Lewis said tiredly. 'If Lacy is there, he'll hear about the jail threat to the woman and — what d'you think he'll do?'

'Hell, goin' on his past performance, I reckon he'll come in an' — ' Suddenly Quinn paused, his face brightening noticeably. 'Aw, shoot, yeah! *He'll come in to help her*!'

'Marvellous!' Dean said quietly, then louder, 'And?'

'We'll be waitin'!'

The rancher sighed, picked up his pen again.

'Very good, Marko — and I'm sure Matthew Lacy will — resist — so keep on your toes.'

'We'll jump him before he knows what hit him, sir!'

Dean sighed heavily. 'Sheriff, I *know* *Lacy* *will* *resist*! Do you understand what I'm saying . . . ?'

After screwing up his face, the lawman began to smile as he nodded. 'I get it, sir! I get it!'

'Just get Lacy! Once and for all. Now go about your business . . . and let me get on with mine.'

* * *

The map Beth had drawn him was excellent, Matt decided, as he spread it across his knees. He was leaning back against a tree, the sorrel grazing on some grass nearby. He looked up from the map, checked her rough sketch of the trees and the area they covered, recognizing where he was right now.

It was late afternoon and the shadows were lengthening, showing a network of draws that could get him down from this high place without being seen and take him up to the State Line. From here, he could just see the winding river just north of the Navajo Reserve which marked the border and, once there —

He stopped his thoughts abruptly.

Once there, he would have a much better chance of escape. He was close enough to even have a choice: Colorado or Utah. The other way would take too long and it only led to Oklahoma or Texas, where he could still be wanted from the trail driving days with Dean.

Texicans were noted for their long memories about such things . . .

'A helluva long way,' he mused. 'Whichever way I go and taking me further and further away from Beth.'

That did it.

He was on the run and it was his own doing, and she had helped him, putting herself in jeopardy — especially with a vindictive idiot like Marko Quinn in charge.

No doubt Dean Lewis would keep an eye on things and step in when and if needed — and he was more of a threat than Marko Quinn could ever be. The lawman could only concentrate on one thing at a time properly, and if he decided Beth had gone too far with her aid to Lacy, then he would likely find it reason enough to . . . what?

What would the fool do to her?

'God only knows!' Lacy said aloud, standing now and folding away the map, stuffing it inside his shirt. He went to the sorrel who looked at him with as much disgust as it was capable of showing as he scooped up the reins.

'Sorry to interrupt your supper, ol' pard, but we're goin' back.'

The horse whinnied and made him work to get into the saddle, but quickly settled after an affectionate pat on the neck and Matt's quiet voice speaking into its ear.

'Let's go, *amigo*. It's a helluva long ride back, I know, but one we've *got* to make! Can't be any other way!'

Even if they nail me, he thought as he worked the horse carefully down the steep rise, the creeping shadows making it dangerous. One wrong step and they would both descend a whole lot faster than was safe.

But there was no other way. Not for him. This was how it had to be.

He was beholden, and the debt had to be paid at whatever cost.

Besides, put more plainly — and *truthfully* — he simply didn't want to leave Beth.

And he wouldn't — even if it meant giving himself up to ensure her safety.

12

WELCOME BACK

The ranch house was in darkness by the time he had returned to a vantage point that allowed him to see the front Flying C yard and corrals, as well as part of one side of the barn, which was merely a blank wall, without either door or windows.

A good place for a posse to hide out in ambush.

Men inside could watch well enough through gaps between the wall planks.

And someone had slipped-up — likely Marko, with his sore head — and left several mounts already saddled, just inside the big corral's gate, in case a pursuit was needed.

Matt smiled to himself as he ducked quickly through the rails, fumbling in his jacket pocket. So, they were waiting for him. *Surprise, surprise! For some-body....*

Maybe he should have ridden straight for town and the jail, but Dean knew Matt well enough to figure he would check out Flying C first.

Now he had to decide: *was* Beth still here? A prisoner in her own ranch? Or had she already been taken to town and locked-up in the jailhouse?

The saddled mounts in the corrals answered that.

Dean Lewis was expecting him to come here. He would have Bronco Cutler already in town hiding out near the jail just to cover all possibilities.

So Matt reckoned Beth was still here, and Dean himself, maybe. Marko Quinn for sure, with a bunch of armed men.

Waiting for him to show.

'Well, I guess I better not disappoint whoever it is,' he murmured, eyes straining to see other patches of darkness that would make good hiding places.

By chance he had hesitated on his arrival about approaching the house from the front, which was where his trail back from the State Line had brought him. Deciding it was too risky, that even Marko Quinn could figure he would not make a frontal approach, he slid back then, crouching, the house now on his left and the big barn on his right.

If he went in from that angle, watchers in either place could possibly see him, but it was too risky to make his way around to the rear of the house.

When in doubt — act! That had been his way during the war and it had worked.

So now, rifle in hand, a cartridge in the breech, he made his move. He skirted the barn, moving well back from the wall, turned behind it to where the worksheds of the ranch were — the area for repairing the buck-boards and Beth's single wagon, a harness rack, an open-front lean-to for spare saddles and other riding gear, a store shed for bagged grain and oats, also a few bags of flour for the kitchen, and, the place he was looking for, the blacksmith's shelter, open-sided, beneath a thatched roof.

As he had hoped the forge was still glowing, the coals banked so it could be started quickly in the morning or at such time as it might be needed.

Crouching, face reflected in the ruddy glow, he blew into the coals several times, poked at them with a rusted length of iron he picked up from the littered floor.

A wave of heat seared his face and he jerked his head back, shucked half-a-dozen cartridges from his belt and scooped a shallow hole with the tool, then used it to pull a layer of glowing coals on top. It was an old trick but one that worked well — and, more importantly, most times.

He got out of there quickly, making his way partly on his belly, rifle at the ready, straining to see the rear door of the house.

He had just focused on it when the first cartridge heated up enough to explode. Coals and ashes showered around him, and then the others went off one by one at ragged intervals. He lay prone: there was no knowing where the lead might fly after each shell was set off.

But by the time the last one had exploded, there were six or seven yelling, chattering men running around the forge area, a rifle firing, followed by a shotgun.

'See him?' someone yelled hoarsely.

'Dunno. Just somethin' movin'.'

'Well, watch where the hell you're shootin'!'

'Keep your head down, you fool!'

'The hell you callin' *fool*! By — '

'*Shut up and look for him, you idiots.*' That was Marko himself.

By then Matt was in the house, the kitchen, spun just in time to see a shadow jump out from beside a tall cupboard, lifting a sixgun.

Matt lunged, bringing the rifle butt

around in a tight arc, crashing it against the man's head. He groaned and fell, and Matt whirled, thumbing back his rifle's hammer as a second dark shape rose from near the door.

'Matt! It's me!'

For a moment he was sure his heart stopped at the sound of Beth's voice, and then he reached out with his left hand, groped for and found her arm, and dragged her against him.

'We have to *move*!' he said hoarsely. 'Hold on to the back of my belt!'

She did so and directed him to another doorway and suddenly they were outside in the cool darkness, close to the corrals. The sounds of running feet mixed with wild yells and the dying echoes of the last bullet in the forge.

'Who the hell's doin' all the shootin'?' someone yelled.

'Who the hell you think!'

'Well, where is he? I don't see nothin'.'

'Aw, Jesus! The corrals! Hear the broncs!'

Men ran for the big corrals now, where the mounts were obviously disturbed, shouting, someone loosing off a couple of wild shots.

By the time they got there, the gates were open and the already saddled horses were running free with cursing men chasing them. The two that managed to catch a mount each leapt for the stirrups — and promptly found themselves writhing on the ground, trying not to get stomped on.

'The son of a *bitch*! He's cut the cinch straps!'

Away on the far side where Matt had the getaway mounts tethered, Beth laughed briefly, out loud.

'You are a — a formidable enemy, Matt Lacy!' she gasped, settling into leather.

'Tell me later!' he snapped, and led the way through the trees, away from the cursing, floundering posse men.

★ ★ ★

All hell had been stirred-up by the rescue and escape of Beth Casey.

Bronco Cutler had been sent down to take full charge and Marko Quinn's anger was enough to cover any form of rising shame he may have felt for allowing Matt to not only take the bait of the captive girl, but to rescue her as well.

'How the hell they ever let you wear that star beats me,' Bronco told Marko. 'I'd shoot you on the spot and get you outa my hair for keeps, was up to me.'

'Well, you ain't got concussion like me, Bronco.' There was a whine in the sheriff's voice and it only served to boost Bronco's anger. 'Doc told me I should be in hospital, not runnin' all over the country chasin' the likes of Matt Lacy! You — you can't stop him! He's — he's way too good an' — '

Marko gave a strangled sound as Bronco's big hand closed around his throat and with a display of strength, the ramrod actually lifted the sheriff six inches off the ground. The lawman struggled and gagged, his face beet-red, and looked to be on the very point of strangling before the brutal ramrod flung him away like so much garbage.

He cringed on the ground, gagging, retching, rubbing frantically at his bruised throat. His eyes held real fear as Bronco raked them all with his bleak stare, one by one. Then, abruptly, he seemed in a better mood now that he had taken out some of his frustration and rage on the man he held responsible for Matt and Beth's escape.

He nudged the lawman roughly with his boot toe.

'Go on, get the hell away to hospital. Now you got a reason to go. You ain't no damn use around here.' Then the ramrod abruptly leaned down and yanked the sheriff's star from his shirt, ripping the cloth. 'An' you've just lost your job — savvy?'

Bronco straightened and pinned the badge to his own shirt pocket, grinned tightly at the two hardcases he had brought with him.

'Suits you, Bronc!' said Alby, the biggest of the two.

'Yeah . . . ? What you reckon, Cliff?'

The second man winked and held up a circled thumb and forefinger. 'Looks good, Bronc. It's — you!'

'Yeah, reckon so.' He glared around suddenly. 'An' *all* you sons of bitches better take note!'

The grins faded quickly. This was the Bronco Cutler they knew best: hard as nails, mean as a pregnant rattler and never losing a minute's sleep over all the men — and women — he had killed since he'd shot his stepfather when he was fourteen years old, then run off to thrust himself upon an unsuspecting world.

'Now this time,' he told them in a voice that crackled with anticipation, his eyes raking the silent posse, 'we *find* Lacy and we *kill* him. The gal — well, leave her to me. Might be a bit of fun left in her yet.'

'I bags seconds, Bronco!' called Alby.

'There ain't no seconds when I'm through with 'em.'

Matt heard most of Bronco's boasting and knew Beth must have, too. He looked at her, and her pale face glowed white in the dark. One hand found his and gripped tightly.

He took it gently, unclasped it and put his other hand in its place. 'Never cramp my gunhand,' he said quietly and felt her give a little shudder. 'This way to my hoss.'

They rode double, her slim arms clasping his waist in a near death grip as he weaved through the trees. When he hesitated, unsure of which way he should go, she called directions quietly in his ear.

'Bear left. Swing in close to that oak, then sharp right. Don't go up that rise! It's studded with rocks and the soil is unstable. Down here . . . *here: Right now or you'll be past the arroyo —* '

'Don't have to yell!'

'Yes I do! I — I'm too breathless to whisper!'

He grunted and kept riding.

If there was any pursuit, he couldn't hear it.

Things had quietened down back there, very abruptly: he wondered if Dean himself had arrived to take over.

If so, it was likely to get mighty lively before they saw the sun-up.

If they saw it . . .

* * *

Matt had been right: Dean Lewis himself had arrived to take over. And he was not in a pleasant mood.

'How in the hell did he manage to escape!' He was in range clothes, of much better quality than almost anyone in the area had seen before.

He wore twin Colts with ivory handles carried in marvellously embossed holsters with genuine silver conchos studding the leather liberally . . . and artistically.

There was no doubt that these were the genuine articles, hand-crafted in

Mexico, or even Spain.

Together with his sand-coloured, wide-brimmed hat with its narrow leather band also studded with half-a-dozen small concho's, Dean Lewis looked more like an advertisement in some Eastern magazine for their idea of what the well-dressed rancher was wearing in the Wild West these days, than a man who could barely make himself act naturally, he wanted to kill so badly.

He raked his hot stare around at the silent, feet-shuffling men in their dusty, worn clothing and their old work-a-day firearms.

'To think I'm paying good money to you ... rabble ... and getting no results for my trouble!' He let that sink in, seeing the eyes lower and look away, in any direction as long as it wasn't towards him. 'Good God! Don't you realize it's — ' He stopped abruptly, frowning. 'No — no, perhaps you don't realize how close it is for the committee to announce their choice of Provisional

Governor, but it is *very* close, take my word for that.'

He planted his hands on his hips, then let them slide so he could grip the ivory handles of his specially made Colts.

The movement brought a new tension and studied silence to the gathering. When he spoke again his voice was hard and seemed to promise all kinds of unspoken threats.

'*I want Matt Lacy — and that blasted woman — dead! Long before then!*'

Everyone there jumped when he shouted the word '*dead!*' It echoed around the trees and the ranch buildings. 'You listening, Matt? *And* your woman!'

He let the words drift off into the night and then spoke softly and reasonably — and that only served to bring frowns of puzzlement to his audience: mood-swinger! Don't rely on gettin' no quick decisions!

'Now it's simple enough, isn't it? Of

course it is — and as an added incentive I will make the person — or persons — responsible for the killings richer by — mmmm — yes, richer by five thousand dollars.' He gave an on-off smile and nodded, amused at the gasps. 'I'll leave you to think about that, but, not for too long, mind! *I want results and pronto!*'

13

LAST STAND

They were in the very rear of an arroyo and the ground rose steeply beyond.

It was too steep to climb, with crumbly ground underfoot as well as a carpet of fist-sized stones.

'Not the best of places,' Matt told Beth with a slight edge to his voice.

'But one that Marko or his men don't know about,' she replied crisply. 'Hopefully, that means that Bronco Cutler doesn't know either.'

He nodded curtly, noting the sharpness of her words. 'Beth, I'm just thinking out loud, not criticizing. Hell, without you, I'd've been lost and likely would've ridden clear back into the midst of those killers before I even noticed.'

She smiled, knowing he couldn't see

it, and suddenly lifted on to her tiptoes just high enough to brush her dry lips across his bristly cheek. 'I think we're both edgy — and no wonder. But let's not waste time, Matt.'

She dodged his effort to hastily return the kiss, and clambered up on to a rock that seemed unsteady, so he moved closer and she rested a hand on his shoulder while staring around into the night.

'I'm just trying to orient myself: it's quite a while since I've been up here. It's hard to make out at night, too. The shadows change the looks of everything. I think we could still get to where I want us to go from here, but we'd have to climb that loose slope behind us. Would the horse make it?'

'He's big and he's game, but his size might set the scree sliding and it'll take us with it.'

'Ye-es. That's what worries me, too. Oh, *hush*!' She spoke quickly and he felt her grip on his shoulder tighten. 'I believe they've out-foxed us! Oh, *damnation*!' She stepped down off the rock and he steadied her. 'I'm sure there are men — on foot — but leading their mounts up the very slope I had in mind for us to use! I can hear them.'

'Me, too, now. It'll be Dean's men, this is his bailiwick as well as yours, remember?'

'Of course! I was foolish enough to overlook that. But he's working on the assumption that I would try for those slopes because there are a couple of small passes in the southern corner, that would bring us to within an easy ride of the river — he must know about them! Which means we'll have to find some other means of getting away!'

'What did you have in mind about the river?'

'Crossing it, of course, a short way upstream. We can easily double back from there, pick up fresh horses at the ranch and head for town.'

He was quiet for a few moments. 'The idea is good . . . '

'But?'

'But having people around won't stop Dean from trying to kill us. It's too close to the time when he might or might not be put forward for the governor's position. He'll be reckless — no! *Ruthless*, Beth. He'll wipe out half the town if he has to. Bronco could do it without missing a draw on his cigarette.'

'I — I never thought about him running amok!'

'He's getting desperate. I've seen him like that before, and it ain't pretty!'

'But where else can we go . . . ? If not to town, I mean?'

'Why don't we make use of the river?'

'What? How?'

'The flow will take us away from the town *and* this area.'

'That's all very well, but we have one horse and no boat! Not even a raft.'

'Why d'you always think of the *problems*!' he said and quickly grinned as her jaw sagged. 'I'm joshin'! Yeah, you're right, but if we didn't take the horse we could find a log and — '

'Oh, don't be silly! I wouldn't even consider asking you to leave that sorrel! You've become very attached to it.'

'Aw, he's a fine horse, but — well, I've had to abandon other broncs I've liked because of circumstances.'

She could hear the reluctance in his voice even as he tried to force himself to believe that turning the sorrel loose was the only option they had.

He turned from patting the horse to look down into the paleness of her face as she glanced up at him.

'We're getting ahead of ourselves: we aren't even at the river yet.'

He smiled and squeezed her arm. 'Very good point. Let's see if we can get across first.'

She nodded and they cautiously moved around the edge of the unstable slope, hoping it might be firmer there.

But she noticed how he shortened the reins as he led the horse, so that he walked closer to the animal. She smiled as she saw his sneaky little pat behind the sorrel's ear.

He really would be sad if they were forced to abandon that big gelding.

★ ★ ★

Dean Lewis gasped raggedly as Bronco Cutler steadied him on a slope that broke away under his weight. The big ramrod just prevented Dean from falling on his face.

'You're sure this is the best way?' Lewis asked between gulps of air.

'The only way,' was Bronco's answer and Dean was willing to accept that — glad to. But he really wouldn't feel safe if he didn't have the big-fisted, brutal, but strongly loyal ramrod with him.

Even here, in this present predicament, Dean thought it was still probably the best day's work he had ever done — the day he had saved Bronco Cutler's life.

It was just after the war ended and he'd heard the cries for help as he made his way across a cratered field, and found Bronco stranded in the bottom of a flooded shell hole near another river, with the muddy water rising fast, already reaching his chest. Bronco yelled up to him that his foot was jammed in the struts of a sunken Gatling gun.

'I'll drown,' Bronco had called up. 'Gimme a hand.'

Dean Lewis never knew why he had replied, facetiously, 'Say 'please'!'

But he saw the shock on Bronco's ravaged face and then the clamping of his teeth, thrusting out his jaw, his eyes hard as bullets.

'Go to hell! I don't beg no man!'

'Then you *will* drown!'

'And I'll curse you, whoever you are, all the way to hell and back!'

Dean had felt a chill of fear within his chest at the man's words. *Here was some determined survivor of the war, but willing to die rather than plead. Oh, he'd ask but he would not plead!*

Right then Dean Lewis knew he could use such a man — for he already had ambitious plans — and could well need a hardcase like this one to back him up, and if the man was beholden to him — well, so much the better.

He had never been sorry for his decision to help the big man out of the flooded crater that day.

Never!

'I have to get back,' Dean rasped now, stumbling even though Bronco held him in a firm grip. 'I must keep track of the . . . candidates . . . and make sure I'm among them. Preferably near, or at the top.'

'Best if we find somethin' to take us down-river, then,' Bronco said. 'I can get us a couple hosses at one of them small spreads down that way. We could be back in town by tomorrow sundown.'

'Too late!' Dean shouted. 'That's *too damn late*! I need to get somewhere I can monitor the council's messages, stay abreast of who . . . who's being considered for the governor's position! And how much of a rival they are.'

Bronco was quiet as he half-carried the out-of-condition, high-living rancher to higher ground.

'There's the relay station over at Buzzsaw, that big lumber camp other side of — '

'I know where Buzzsaw is! And, yes. That's an excellent idea, Bronco. But can we get there in time?'

'If that's what you want, we'll do it — even if I have to sprout wings and fly.'

Ignoring the last part, Dean Lewis smiled. *Yes. If there was a way to do it, Bronco Cutler would find it* — at any cost.

*   *   *

They stopped and stared at the river.

It flowed by at a fast rate, actually on descending ground here, which added to the force of the current. Beth had a look of alarm on her face as she turned quickly to Matt.

'I — I didn't realize it flowed at such

a rate! I spent most of my river time upstream, near the ranch, where it swings across my land, but I didn't realize this slope had added such a strong force to the flow.'

'Don't take much of a drop in the land to form a few rapids or small waterfalls, long as the volume is there,' he explained. 'They all add to the current.'

Beth was frowning. 'I — I'm not a great lover of rivers — almost drowned once. Oh, it was years ago now, but I've always remembered that awful feeling of going under, swallowing water instead of air . . . '

He was looking at her soberly. 'You're not exactly keen to float down on any damn log, are you?'

'I — I would prefer not to have to *float* on anything, if you want the truth.'

'That's what I want. But if we don't use the river — well, you know this country better than me. Is there a way we can get out of here, on the sorrel?'

'I think so, but . . . ' She gave him a

wan smile. 'We still need to cross the river to pick up the trail.'

He sighed. 'Well, I'm used to that spot between a rock and a hard place, but I've been alone most times, only had myself to worry about.'

'You don't need to worry about me. I may be somewhat less than courageous, but — you inspire a confidence in me, Matt Lacy.' Her smile widened, and she spread her hands. 'I'm literally in your hands!'

'Might have to wait a little for that to be true,' he said quietly, 'but if you're game, we'll see if we can find a way to get across. Shouldn't need that big a log, just for the two of us.'

Her smile faded as she detected the unwilling but noticeable regret in his tone as he glanced at the patient sorrel when he spoke those last few words.

It would have to be left behind, of course.

*   *   *

Marko Quinn was feeling left out. He knew he hadn't performed well, but that was just one of those things.

He knew he was never top-notch, not at anything — the whole of his life had been the same.

But he had managed to get through, found the necessary effort, and still had some good times in between.

This time, though, it had really hit him where he lived when that skunk Bronco Cutler had put him down in front of everyone! *Everyone who mattered to Marko, leastways.*

But now, Marko was ready for payback: so he no longer had any stake in this deal, Bronco having stripped him of his badge, huh?

Unfortunately, the man would soon enough get Dean's approval: he could do little wrong in Lewis's eyes.

And where would that leave Marko?

Out on a limb with nothing but a long, long drop before him. *Like Hell!*

He would have his reckoning — and right soon!

14

MATT'S FAREWELL

They were set to cross the river.

Matt had already retrieved a medium-sized log and a couple of long, slim branches for poles. It would easily carry them both across the placid, oval pool they had come to about a mile below the rapids.

They hadn't seen any sign of pursuit so far.

Beth sat morosely on the log where they had drawn it up on the bank, watching as Matt unsaddled the sorrel, paused when taking off the reins, edging closer, kind of holding its head against him. She had no doubt that he was saying his farewell to the animal — saying his *private* farewell.

Then, suddenly, he stepped back and cracked the rein ends over the startled horse's rump. He flung his arms wide, yelling just the once. The animal shied away, whinnying.

'I'll come look for you, *amigo*,' she heard him say and although she listened closely, she could not detect any huskiness in his voice.

To her, it seemed as though he had come to terms with the inevitable parting.

*　*　*

Matt had deliberately delayed as long as he could, so that there was daylight for the proposed river crossing, and could see the change in Beth right away when the sun's first rays outlined the range: she felt much better now she could see things more clearly.

Then she put the back of a hand to her mouth, but it didn't fully cover her gasp as she saw, quite plainly, the surging, frothing waters of the river, roiling in a small set of rapids: she quickly stepped back as spray reached her.

'Oh, dear God!' she said quietly, and Matt thought his arm would go numb if she gripped him any harder. 'I — I don't think I could commit myself to . . . that!'

'Rapids slow down a river, Beth. It may not look like it, but they do. Oh, I don't mean the whole damn river, but — say — half a mile below these rapids, you could expect to find another pool placid enough to reflect the sky and the birds and the trees.'

'You're just trying to make me feel better. Well, there's no need. I'm not entirely a fool, you know. I can see for myself how dangerous it is . . . '

'Up here, yes,' he agreed. 'But we'll keep on down stream along the bank until we find where the river's lost the momentum built up by the rapids. It'll be much calmer.'

'Look at your horse!' she cried suddenly.

The sorrel, which had followed them, was obviously perturbed at the violence of the river, forelegs propped, eyes rolling, nostrils quivering as he snorted and started to back-up.

Matt stroked the muzzle, spoke gently, following slowly as it continued to back away.

And then it began to slow and stopped tossing its head so wildly. He rubbed its muzzle, tweeked both ears, stroked it under the stiffened jaw which he felt slowly relaxing.

'He'll be fine. We don't know each other so well yet. But I've just shown him I'm not expecting him to leap into that — maelstrom. Downstream it ought to be different and he'll be confident again. He'll follow on the bank.'

She stared at him, and even stroked the horse, feeling that it had stopped quivering now.

'You . . . you'll never just abandon this horse, will you?'

'Don't see any need to.'

'But when we come to cross . . . ?'

'I'll swim him across. You can hold his mane, on the downstream side, and his body'll protect you from the main force, which will be nothing like it is here.'

She stared soberly at him for a long minute and then gave him a half-smile. 'Like I said, you won't leave him!'

'Nor you.'

She looked into his rugged face — and had no answer to that . . . or at least nothing she wanted to put into words right then. Later — well, she would think about just how she was going to demonstrate her appreciation.

★　★　★

The crossing was not without its drama. Beth lost her grip on the wet mane, going under briefly, spluttering, gulping, on the verge of panic.

But Matt's powerful right arm was there to support her and after some more struggling, she settled down.

'Sorry, but I really don't like deep water.'

'We'll be in the shallows soon and

you can put your feet down and touch bottom.'

It was only minutes before this happened. As he helped her up, the sorrel whinnied, stepping briskly along the bank they had just left, pausing to turn back, whistling and snorting as it tried to convey its displeasure to Matt.

'I'll be back for you! That's a promise.'

He gave a small start when he turned and saw her staring at him, frowning.

'Do you believe he understood that?'

'Well, I guess he don't speak American but he can tell by the tone of my voice whether it's good words or bad — see?'

The sorrel pawed the ground and gave a short whinny, then just stood there looking at Matt Lacy with big, almost dreamy eyes.

'Heavens! You do have some real communication with that animal, don't you?'

'Reckon we savvy each other to a certain extent — plan to get to know him one helluva lot better.'

She smiled and stepped closer, groping for his hand.

And then there was a rifle shot across the river.

He whirled just as the sorrel reared and pawed the air, giving a short, shrill whinny before it crashed to the ground on its side, legs kicking, head rising and falling . . .

'Oh! God *no! Please* — *no!*'

Matt may not have heard Beth's cry of anguish. He was frozen, watching the sorrel's death throes, unable to breathe briefly, stunned, trying to accept this sudden transition from life to sudden death.

He had seen plenty of it in the war, of course, and had even been close to some of his mounts, but never as close as he had felt with the sorrel.

He was already in a gunman's crouch, Colt in hand, having no recollection of it getting there. The girl was saying something, her words distorted by sobs, and, strangely, he had a thought that she was crying for *him* as well as the horse.

Then a voice echoed out of the trees: 'Well, damn me, Lacy! Shot musta went wild and hit your hoss, I see. Ah, well, there're plenty more in the world. But . . . I have to be moving along now, so *adios*!'

It was Bronco Cutler.

Matt almost choked as he tried to answer the man but the words wouldn't force themselves out. He triggered two shots, knowing at once that the man was out of range. Then, as Beth stepped back at the terrible look on his face, he said flatly, 'Stay here! Get behind the logs and *stay there*!'

'But where're you — '

He was already on the log that had floated them across, pushing his rifle through his belt. He sat astride, then, clumsily using the pole.

She called his name twice — three times. 'Come back!'

He didn't look up, concentrated on reaching the other side. A rifle shot whiplashed from within the line of trees and the bullet chewed splinters from the front of the log.

He dropped into the water which was about waist deep here, holding the rifle so it wouldn't get wet. Crouching, he threw himself against the bank, as close as he could, twisted, and fired three rapid shots into the trees.

He had noticed where Bronco's gunsmoke was rising and he was close with his volley, heard the killer shout in alarm as lead churned about him.

Then Matt vaulted up on to the bank, rolled towards a line of brush, and abruptly reversed the move as Bronco rose to get a better shot at where he thought Matt was.

But Matt Lacy twisted as he dropped back over the bank, landed on one knee, rifle lifting to his shoulder and there — clearly in the foresight — was the ramrod, poised to shoot, not realizing *he was also a target*.

Matt's bullet burned Bronco's hip, spinning him halfway around with sudden violence. Even as his leg was smashed out from under him, Bronco's arms clawed air above his head in some kind of involuntary, convulsive movement as he fought for balance: for a moment it appeared he was dancing.

But it was a mighty *painful* dance, and he knew he could expect no compassion or mercy from Lacy now he had killed the man's horse. Panic became a live thing within him, wrenching at his gut, putting the acid of fear flooding into his throat: it was not a new experience but one he hadn't had for a very long time.

Sobbing without realizing it, he clenched his teeth, somehow managed to jam a kerchief over his blood-spurting thigh, and started to flounder in an effort to crawl away.

He dropped behind some rocks, screened by brush, scrubbed streaming sweat from his dusty face and brought his rifle up and around, but the movement set the bushes swaying, giving away his position.

Matt's rifle raked the area instantly and the unusual sensation of true fear surged through Bronco Cutler as he tried to push to his knees, in an effort to locate Matt.

Then there was a loud — *close* — crashing of the brush and Matt was hurtling at him. The rifle butt clipped Bronco hard enough to dislodge his hat and, falling, he somehow managed a somersault and tossed dirt at Matt's face. Lacy ducked, blinked wildly, and *threw his rifle* as Bronco lifted his own weapon.

There was luck in Matt's throw and it tore Bronco's Winchester from his grasp. Before the guns reached the ground, Matt's fists were hammering at the killer. Bronco ducked and weaved — more at home with his fists than guns, it seemed — and he landed a couple of rib-benders that had Lacy back-pedalling.

Bronco lunged and Matt got his arms about the thick shoulders. They wrestled, stumbled, swore, right on the edge of the drop. Bronco twisted his head and suddenly yelled in panic, 'Not the river! I — I can't swim! Oh, Jesus!'

'Time you learned,' Matt gritted, twisted the man and rammed a shoulder hard into his back.

Bronco yelled wildly and fell, groping hands ripping part of the collar of Matt's shirt. He yelled and thrashed all the way down until the water closed over his head. Matt stumbled and crawled to the edge of the drop, looked down ... in time to see the killer swimming strongly towards a sloping shelf of sand about ten yards away.

So the son of a bitch had lied!

Dripping, Bronco scrambled ashore, stood awkwardly and flicked a mocking salute in Matt's direction.

'I'm a fast learner, huh?' he called triumphantly, laughing.

Matt snatched up his rifle, rammed the butt into his shoulder and triggered. Bronco stopped laughing, dived headlong and the bullet kicked sand into his face. Alarmed now, he stumbled to his feet and floundered up the slope.

Matt fired again, this time taking aim carefully, and Bronco's right leg jumped out from under him as if jerked by a wire. He screamed, grabbed the bloody wound and rolled and thrashed about, churning sand into a cloud.

'Kneecap's gone, Bronco!' Matt called down. 'Let's see how well you swim now.'

But Bronco Cutler had no interest at all in swimming or anything else right now, except the unbearable pain consuming his entire body. His sobs were interspersed with a string of terrible curses.

'Wonder if my horse thought the same about you when you shot him, you miserable bastard!'

Then, at a sound behind him, Matt whirled, bringing the smoking rifle around swiftly.

It was Beth — dishevelled, white face screwed up in horror as Bronco's screams of agony rang across the slope.

She clapped her hands over her ears

and turned away.

'Oh, Matt! Matt! Stop this — *please*! I — I know he did a terrible thing, but ... this is — I — I never thought you ... ' Her voice trailed off as she saw the cold, unfeeling look on his face.

Without a word, he lifted the rifle again and fired two swift shots.

Bronco's screams abruptly stopped.

Matt pushed past Beth as she stared at Bronco's huddled body. Getting her balance again, she called his name and started after him. He paused as she ran up.

'I'm sorry you had to see that side of me, Beth.'

'Yes, so — so am I, but if it's a part of you, I guess I should know about such things,' she stammered.

She reached for his left arm, remembering he had told her never to cramp his gun arm.

'Matt, I guess by your way of thinking — and under the circum-stances — it could be called justified. I think I can understand that, but I wouldn't like to see it ever again.'

'Not likely to,' he told her in clipped tones, and she saw he was staring at the sorrel. 'But it will still be there somewhere . . . '

'Oh, Matt!' Her compassion and effort to understand were plain in her voice and face. He said nothing and after a few moments, she asked, 'What will you do now?'

'Dean started this. Up to me to end it.'

'I — I know you see it that way but he'll surround himself with many men like Bronco Cutler — far worse probably!'

'I'd expect that.'

'How can you be so calm about it? You might be killed!'

'Or Dean might.'

'Well, yes. I suppose, I . . . *hope* you're right, of course, but — ' Her next words came with a rush. 'Don't go after Dean Lewis with a gun! Please, Matt!'

'What d'you want me to do?' He was plainly puzzled.

'What he's been afraid you were going to do all along.'

He frowned. 'What? Tell how he's lived a lie all this time?' He shook his head. 'Never prove a thing now.'

'You wouldn't have to. The accusation would be enough. That's all it would need: the suspicion it *could* be true! It'd be enough so he would never be considered as governor of anywhere! With his ego and arrogance, a slur like that will destroy him.'

Matt's frown deepened and he stared steadily at her, weighing her words.

'And if he's got any sense at all,' she continued, 'he'll never allow anything to happen to you, because it would be seen as an attempt on his part to stop you talking.' She sobered then. 'Even so, it would be very dangerous.'

'And very much a real, damn pleasure! I like your idea, Beth.'

He reached for her and she came willingly to him, her heart hammering as she clutched him: he could almost *feel* the relief flooding through her.

She knew he could do this.

Knew he would do it — for her.